In memory of those we have lost.

Special thanks to my wife for putting up with my crazy ass.

Big shout out to those who have helped me along the way;
Marnie Macrae, Ava Brody, Aleron Kong, Geneva Agnos,
and countless more.

Nobody has to suffer alone.

Contents

The Unreliable Narrator

My name is Sgt. Rodney James LeClaire, US Army (Ret.), and I will be your unreliable narrator. If it sounds odd to you that I refer to myself as sergeant or include the bit about US Army, I assure you, it is odd to me too. I find that it very much plays into my identity, and, therefore, this story today. I toss back and forth as to whether or not I should include it as part of my signature block. The truth is, I don't know. Is this what I am? And if so, is this all I am? All I will be? Furthermore, how do I fit myself into a story? There are things that you don’t find in movies or books; crippling self-doubt or anxiety. Self-deprecating humor used liberally to cover deep psychological wounds. I cannot be the hero in my own story if I am not even sure if I am the good guy, much less a hero. Drama aside, I aim to present you with the unvarnished truth. I will let you pour over my life as I expose every dark fact, every hidden pain. You will share in my triumphs and suffer in my defeats. You, my dear reader, will be presented with the singular opportunity to judge me in a way that no other ever will.

We now come to the second part of my opening statement. I am unreliable. I will stretch the truth, avoid the truth, and lie to you. Understand this is not in an effort to paint myself in a better light, rather, I would never let something as paltry as the truth get in the way of a good story. As if I were Quixote tilting at windmills, some of the story exists only in my head. Some of it, however, is the God's honest truth. The rest, and majority of the following, is probably somewhere between the two. If you only believe one thing, it is that you are better off not trusting me. I aim only to tell my side of the story. If any of the parties affiliated with or mentioned in the following story want their opinions heard, well, hell, let them write their own goddamn book. Also, it should be mentioned that there will be foul language, followed by and preceding foul situations. There are some times in life that can only be greeted and properly expressed by the word... FUCK. As in "Fuck me, did I just run over that guys face?" Followed by, "Fuck, I did, now it is stuck in the tire." If, in fact, you are able to say these sentences without the usage of the word fuck, you, sir, or madam, are far more fucked up than I.

So, now that the preface is out of the way, let me start by telling you everything I write is one hundred percent unadulterated truth. I will never lie or deceive you, oh wise reader, as I am counting on your magnanimity to grant me absolution. Good, bad, and in-between, I lay myself bare for your judgement. At some point in time, I may even tell you the story I have been promising. I suppose we should start at the beginning.

In the beginning, God created the heavens and the earth. Fast forward some years later, and I was born. Now, I wish it had been on some dark and stormy night, emerging into this world with a cry in time with the last stroke of midnight. The darkness pierced intermittently by bolts of lightning. Sage and the smell of fresh rain hanging in the air. But I wasn't. I was born at 4pm on a Tuesday afternoon. I do not remember the weather firsthand but have read that it was overcast. I was in a hospital anyway so who gives a fuck. Weather is for people who are outdoors.

Now, I am told there is a certain flow to stories. A beginning, a middle, and an end. That I should introduce those who share my story and provide backstory and context. This way, you can relate to the main character and auxiliary characters' struggles and understand who they are and why they react the way they do when the time for action comes. With this approach, you can really take time developing a deep personal connection, that way you can feel joy at their triumphs and sadness at their inevitable deaths. Stories need to happen in chronological order so we can watch a character grow and develop. The first thing you will learn about me (or, hell, maybe even the third thing by now) is I ain't no damn character, and this isn't a fairytale. Soo... fuck 'em and fuck you if Y'all can't take a joke. I will start wherever I damn well please. Thank you.

It was hot. Not like let's go to the beach hot, but like I am going to die hot. The kind of heat you feel when you forget your shoes and have to walk barefoot over asphalt mid-summer. Except on your whole body. In order to keep you cool, the army prescribes an undershirt, a long sleeve jacket, fifteen pounds of body armor carrier for your chest, filled with ten pounds of armor, two big samurai looking pads for your arms, two five pound pieces of armor to fit at your sides, and a seven pound helmet. You know, something to really trap in the cool. You also carry a rucksack or assault bag. This makes it easier for you to carry copious amounts of water, which you will sorely need, propaganda flyers, which you will not, and, of course, life preserving ammunition and weaponry. Democracy brought to you 5.56 millimeters at a time.

The next thing to describe is the smell. You know that smell that happens when you are wearing said equipment in aforementioned weather and have only showered with a water bottle or baby wipes for three months... that is the smell that you are praying to breathe in as you are walking down the streets. Open trenches lay to either side that the locals use as latrines and a place for animal offal and by product after slaughtering them for market. All baked at 120 degrees for maximum potency. Add in the fact that deodorant was not a social norm in this part of the world, even the memory of the smell makes me gag now.

The dust was thick and heavy in the air. Clouds of acrid smoke drift across the desert. Trash and cooking fires burning in equal measures. The air was gritty. A literal dusting applied to everyone and everything. It hits the back of your throat, coating your tongue and teeth with a thin film of grime. You tried to spit, but the heat has sapped your moisture. This dust covers everything. What should be vibrant colors seem muted.

Everything was dull brown or other earth tones. The harshness of the light removed life from the things it painted.

I know what you're thinking... the perfect setting for a hike. Or as the Army likes to call it—a patrol. Some minor things I ought to mention for those of you who can't put two and two together. It is Afghanistan. I am at war. The population hates us. Even if they don't manage to kill us, there was a massive amount of leftover mines from the Soviets which blow up on a semi regular basis that can and will kill us.

Which brings me to my first tangent. Also, incidentally, to the first person in the story who isn't me. He was a local national who had a job on our small combat outpost as a janitor. While walking to work one day, he'd had the misfortune of stepping on a landmine and losing both of his legs. A medic had managed to save his life, but as it turned out, Afghanistan was woefully short on top notch prosthetics. As a result, he'd received two wooden replacements that were of slightly different lengths, this gave him a rather peculiar gait. On hard surfaces, this was coupled with the tapping of wood prosthetics. Hence, our name for him—Happy Feet. This, more than any other thing, should give you an idea of what passes for humor in a war-time environment.

But I digress. So, like any great drinking story, no shit, there we were, in the middle of Afghanistan, doing a patrol. We were in a column formation. For those of you who were not in the military, this just looks like people walking in a fucking line. Now we have reached a point in the story where other people have to be involved. Seeing as I have not spoken to these people and have little to no idea what they are doing and what ramifications will be in their personal life if said stories were brought to light, I will refer to them in such a way that everyone who was there will know who they are but everyone who was not are probably shit out of luck. We were led both literally and figuratively by Staff Sgt. Rod. He was followed by Pvt. Pistols and myself then specialist gunner LeClaire. Rounding out our team was Spc. Chile. Now Chile was not only a passive aggressive whiny fuck, but also the driver of our vehicle, so, after a short but heated debate, it was determined that he got to stay with the truck. As such, he plays a very little part in this story. I am not bitter, I swear.

Other people followed us in line, but I'm not going to mention them, because frankly, I don't give a shit. There was an interpreter, or a terp as they are affectionately known. Fun fact, most of the time, our patrols occurred in column formation. This is because the whole country was mined, and you never were quite sure where it was safe to walk. By walking in a single file line, we limited our exposure to just the person in the front. One of the things Hollywood often screws up, when we walk in this line, we are not nut to butt. That would eliminate any benefit of being single file in the first place. If the first person in a normal single file line stepped on a mine, the next six people would die. Rest assured, there is a healthy distance between soldiers. I would say five meters, but as you dear reader and most of our soldiers are probably American, nobody knows what the fuck a meter is. But, rest assured, there was some sort of variance of space between each individual, limiting the casualties taken in the event of an explosion.

Our terp came to the front and started to talk to some local nationals, routine stuff, he asked them who they were and told them who we were. Then one of the locals just booked it. Like full dead-on sprint out of nowhere booked it. Like there were thirteen tired hot sweaty Americans armed for bear and out for blood after him. As any good leader would do, Rod took action. He sprang forward and ran after this guy. Then over his shoulder yelled for me and Pistols to go over this hill while he followed the local directly by running a small goat path meandering around the base of the hill. Now I am not a runner in the best of conditions, and those were not the best of conditions. Me and Pistols raced up the mound following a small animal path, slipping on what I hoped was just goat shit the whole way. By the time we were halfway up, I was sucking wind like I was in a puking CrossFit level workout, when I heard the sound of gunfire. I want to make a sound noise here like bang, bang, bang or *BRRRRT*, but nothing I put up here will accurately describe gunfire. Either you have heard it, or you have not. Three rounds burst out, interrupting my ragged breaths and causing echoes through the landscape.

Oh shit. Oh SHIT! Was that an AK? Is Rod shot? I got that stupid strength only given to adrenaline-fueled grandmothers lifting cars off babies and bounded up the rest of the hill. Usain Bolt fast. Adrenaline coursed through my system. Weapons and gear be damned, no one was going to die while waiting on me.

I crested the top of the hill only to look out and find Rod crumpled down toward the base of the hill some hundred meters down the steep and rocky terrain from me. I yelled toward Pistols and told him to set up his M249 light machine gun and pull security while I went down to check on Rod. I was afraid I was too late. I'd failed. In my mind, I was handing a folded flag to his wife and trying to explain to his daughters how their dad was a hero.

At this point, I was dashing downhill. Weapon slung at my back on a three-point sling, the barrel rhythmically slapping at the back of my knees. Both arms pumped with the fury of an angry god as I sought to use the air to pull myself closer, faster. I saw Rod start to rise. Did I make it in time? Is he okay? What the fuck happened?

Now the official story was that Rod returned fire and took up a defensive position. What had actually happened is he had placed his weapon on burst instead of safe. So not only was the gun turned “on” it was on “turbo mode.” While running, he had tripped and pulled the trigger, demonstrating his lack of ability to use his secondary safety, his finger, showering the hilltop that Pistols now occupied with lead. He had lost track of the local who’d avoided the hilltop because, as I only found out after the fact, it was heavily mined. The interpreter had caught up with the terrorist hiding amidst a group of construction workers. Somehow, the bad individual had grouped up with more bad guys…? They’d stopped running at the sound of gunshots. These assholes threatened a group of local nationals with violence if the workers did not comply. In short order, we were able to discern the bad guys from the probably soon to be bad guys and detained them. As it turned out, several were known enemy combatants and were on a watchlist. For our roles in detaining these individuals, me and Pistols were awarded a certificate of achievement.

In a nutshell, short walk, small talk, dude runs, so we follow, Rod trips, shooting the hill we were climbing, then there are four terrorists, medals for everyone. I have no idea why. Moral of the story I guess, if someone runs, follow them. Thus ends my first Afghan misadventure.

Shots

Ah, my intrepid reader. I ask that you gather your resolve. For today, we push onward into uncharted territory. I present to you a tale so harrowing, so jaw dropping, so mind numbing, it haunts me to this very day.

I awoke with a start. The sheet clung to my sweaty skin. I could hear my heart pounding. There is no discernable reason for this unsettling. Perhaps a premonition for things to come. I shook my head as if movement would ward off the impending doom. A glance toward the clock told me it was 3:03 am. Mission at oh-five-thirty, I went back to bed.

The alarm rang. In my state of diminished alertness, I lazily reached over to shut it off. Time to get up. Forty-five minutes to shit, shower, and shave. Twenty minutes to grab chow. Fifteen minutes to load up the truck. For those just joining our story—shame on you. Go back and read the first one. The morning progressed smoothly. Ammo loaded, gun prepped, computer online. Comms were clear. Those of you who aren't battle hardened veterans of the Iraq or Afghanistan wars might need some clarification. This meant I had prepped the truck by turning everything on and hooking up weapons systems. The radio (read SINGARS person to person radio not AM/FM) was able to connect to other people. I operated a CROWS, or crew remote operated weapons system. Basically a .50 cal machine gun hooked up to a camera operated by joystick. 12x zoom. In essence, I have played the most badass game of call of duty ever. Hooking the gun up to the camera and ensuring everything was calibrated took the majority of my prep time. There are several wires that needed connecting and restraining bolts to ensure that the gun's recoil did not knock it off of the platform.

The location was Gardez, Afghanistan. Ssgt. Rod gave the briefing. Our mission was to collect census data and to provide a presence patrol in downtown Gardez. We would depart at 1000 hours and finish at 1900 hours. Each step of our mission was carefully outlined. Every eventuality accounted and planned for. All except for one. Side note—in order to make a 1000 hrs. SP, or starting point, everyone had to be ready to go by 0530 hrs. Which meant wake up at 0400 hours. If this doesn't make any sense to you, I would strongly advise you to avoid the military.

We arrived at checkpoint alpha without a hitch. Almost too easy in hindsight. Murphy's Law just setting me up for the big one. Our interpreter offered to go to the market nearby and grab us hamburgers. Now, a hamburger in America consists of a beef patty sandwiched in between two buns. Oftentimes, they include lettuce or tomato and some sort of condiment. In Afghanistan, a hamburger apparently consisted of goat wrapped in foot bread, seasoned with dirt, and covered in a shit flavored gravy.

Poor food choices aside, checkpoints alpha, bravo, and charlie went smoothly. A little more background is in order, I suppose. At these checkpoints, we stopped all military age males and took biometric and personal data. Think—stop and frisk, except it's stop and take scans of your eyeballs, fingerprints, and names of you and your family members. Anything to try and connect you to past or future crimes. These checkpoints were a perfect place to be attacked. Suicide vests, vehicle borne improvised explosive devices, and sniper fire were just some of the perils we faced.

In light of those dangers, I remained ever vigilant, standing guard over my fellow soldiers as I panned my machine gun back and forth. As much as I want to leave that image of the lone sentinel in vigil, I should probably clarify what this actually looked like. I was sitting in a chair slightly too small for me, staring at a twelve-inch monitor. Joystick in one hand, knock off energy drink in the other. In between drinks I would take time to adjust the A.C. or eat peanut M&Ms. God it felt good to be a gangster.

Meanwhile, the rest of my team was out in the soothing hundred-and-ten-degree-heat, enjoying the sights and, more importantly, smells of a culture that didn't believe in deodorant. Such was my burden. After several hours of comparative luxury, more suffering. The powers that be called RP, or end of mission. After a short trip, we made it. Safely on base, we held a Call of Duty tournament. I got first place. Good day.

Quit thinking you know what is going to happen. Read this chapter again any time you think you know me or know war. In real life, most missions aren't firefights or people dying.

Special forces makes up like one percent of the military and ninety percent of the movies and books. I aim to tell you the story of an average soldier. Most who have been downrange will have experienced these events, or something similar. So, turn off your preconceived notions and go on this journey with me. I will need you awake and unbiased in stories ahead.

Entropy

By now, dearest reader, you should have a handle on my prose and style. You think you know me. You think you have a concept of my character. A little narcissistic, a healthy dose of sarcasm, and of course a heaping helping of humor. I can assure you that whatever preconceptions or notions you might have of me are wrong. As you have shown me your fidelity by staying with me this far, I shall reward you with a story of my own virtue faithfulness. You might call it grit, you might just call it my own particular brand of stupid, but for better or worse, this is me. Like all the stories I have told, this one is one hundred percent true, except for those few parts that are complete lies, or the other parts which are stretched or skewed.

It happened on the way to Jaji, a small town with a smaller police precinct way up in the Hindu Kush mountain range of Afghanistan. My squad and I were set to make the four-hour drive from Combat Outpost Herrera to meet up with the Afghan border patrol in order to search out insurgents sneaking in from Pakistan. For this mission, I was in the turret of an MRAP. MRAP is military speak for a big ass truck with a big ass gun strapped to the roof. This particular truck did not have a CROWS, shame. As a gunner, I enjoyed the benefit of putting a size ten ass on a size two sling, half in the truck and half out of the truck. If, for some reason, you are unable to imagine this and are unable to use the internet to look up things you don’t understand, just quit now, it will only get worse.

So, my truck was second in a big line of trucks, trundling up the mountain. Second place in line was the sweet spot. You should be safe from landmines, but close enough that the dust that was kicked up from the massive vehicles wasn't yet thick enough to choke and blind you. The trucks were about twelve feet across, the road, and I use that term loosely, was about eleven feet across. This detail played a very important part in the upcoming story. About three hours in, we were well up the mountain. We hugged the inside wall, driving on the shoulder as the right side dropped off into a small cliff. We slowed down for a particularly narrow part of the road. The first truck makes it through. As our truck drove the pass, it started slipping. Hemingway once wrote that it happened gradually, then suddenly (bankruptcy in his work, truck falling off a cliff in mine). The truck fell in slow motion. I stared out at the perfect azure blue sky, the world tilting in slow motion. My truck was gone, I floated through the air... then a stop, and blackness. I awoke in a field. The plants were tall enough that I couldn't see. Where was I? I looked down. I had my pistol. I was wearing my armor. I was in Afghanistan. We were on patrol. Someone was yelling. They were yelling a name. My name. I was here. I yelled. In the plants. What plants? I looked around. This looked familiar. I couldn't place it. Wait, I could. I had seen this before. Leonardo DiCaprio had been here. In a field of the same plants. That didn't make sense. Why would Leonardo be in Afghanistan. Wait, that was a movie. What was that movie? The Beach. The one with the marijuana fields. I was in a field of six-foot-high marijuana plants, actual Afghan Kush.

I had died. I was positive. My stoner friends were right, and heaven was a field of six-foot-high Mary Jane. My sergeant continued yelling, I guessed I wasn't dead. I stumbled toward the voice. I tripped over a piece of metal. I recognized this metal. It was my metal. More specifically, it was the metal I had put on the truck earlier that day. The .50 caliber machine gun had shorn its pin that held it on the truck and now lay in the dirt at my feet. The barrel, half inch thick on either side, was bent at a thirty-degree angle. I picked up the gun in both hands. It immediately dropped out of my left. I threw it over my shoulder and headed to the truck. The truck was laying on its side at the base of a small cliff. From where we were, we could see that the edge of the road was dug out. Someone had been making a tunnel into the side. For nefarious purposes, or for a drainage ditch, we would never know.

Other people in the truck faced minor injuries. Spc. East had a box of MREs break a cord and hit him in the arm. A lot of stuff happened. Some recovery. Extra people came out to save us. Yadda yadda. Didn't matter. Immaterial to the story, or at least to my story. We made it back to the base. The medic examined me. I pass the TBI test, the check for concussion or other brain injuries. A quick look at my wrist. He said it was sprained. Gave me ibuprofen and suggested I drink water and keep it wrapped in an ace bandage.

Eleven more months of deployment went by. Firefights, missions, and patrols. Enemies are captured, and friends die. The pain in my wrist was now accentuated by a clicking noise.

Medic didn't care. Made it back to Germany. The wrist that had been sprained had really been broken. Almost a year working on a broken wrist. The bone had decayed in my body. Grafts, plates, screws. Three surgeries. I lost my job as a military police officer. I could no longer meet physical requirements.

I have regained some use in my wrist. However, I will never do another pullup, pushup, or bench press. I will never play catch with my son. I traded my health and wellness for twenty-two hundred dollars a month. My physical injuries did not stop me from finishing mission. I feel broken. I feel less of a man. Maybe if I had made a bigger deal about my injuries, I could have gotten proper medical treatment. Maybe if I had made myself known. I blame myself. In the long scheme of things, my physical ailments were among the least of the pain I suffered.

Enough sappy shit. Everyone has their cross to bear. I walked away. I get paid. My life is great compared to those who didn't. I feel good. I can't complain.

Shit

Esteemed reader, today we devolve. For the purpose of clarity, we are going to resort to the lowest form of humor imaginable. Something that has been making children laugh since the beginning of time. We will be discussing feces. More specifically—my feces. So, I strongly advise you to buck up and drive on. If this sort of thing isn't for you, then fuck off. The real story isn't always pretty. As a matter of fact, it is shit covered. Afghanistan is the perfect setting for this story. Shit country with shit people and a shit war where I can do my shit job.

Side note, Afghan people do not operate in the same way as you or I in regard to sanitation and hygiene. A lot of them defecate in places of convenience for the individual as opposed to places designated for this bodily function. I know in my heart of hearts that they go in places that make sense for them in their culture. That said, it is abso-fucking-lutely disgusting. In rivers, in fields, unused rooms of buildings, these guys shit everywhere.

Returned from mission. Hot, sweaty. My ACU top and undershirt were wet to the touch after I removed my body armor. The night had done wonders in cooling down the air, but my body seemed to still be playing catch up. I grabbed a water and a crystal light lemonade packet. These things made my deployment. Lemonade on the go. Fucking amazing. Somebody needs to contact the guy who created those single serve packets and give him a goddamn medal. Lord knows I would if I could.

I sat down on my twin mattress. My M240b machine gun was lying on the bed next to me. This is like the middle brother between the .50 cal and the 5.56 caliber bullet of the M249 machine gun. I took off my shirt and top and hung them from a knob hanging on the backside of my door made for this purpose. I knew from prior experience that it was best to hang them out until you could get to the laundry. In a bag, they just seemed to fester. Now that I was in some semblance of comfort, I started the laborious task of cleaning my crew-served weapon. Crew served, being somewhat of a misnomer, as my entire military career, I had been the only one carrying, cleaning, and firing the "crew-served weapon." The weapon got disassembled into its base components, and then I hand cleaned each piece individually. There were a lot of pieces. It was a labor of love though. Not love for the weapon, rather love for myself. Each piece of my kit needed to remain in top shape for the next mission. I have known people whose weapons had failed them at a critical juncture. Mine would not (except of course that one time when it did, but that is another story altogether).

About halfway through, I got a tingle in my intestines. The tingle quickly turned into a kick in the guts. I could barely stand up. I was in so much pain. Luckily, the bathroom was set up as a trailer thirty feet outside the door of my hooch (read building I live in). I exited my room, grabbing my 9mil and padlocking my door. Bathroom emergency or not, no one was stealing my weapons or trying to take me without a fight. I risked a fast step, then resorted to a sort of half bent over slow twisty walk, that you typically see in children who have to pee. Oh god, it hurt. I opened the first stall I came to. I drop my pants while sitting down. Or at least I was trying to sit down. My body was just about in the shape of an L laying upside-down. My pants were around my thighs, and my ass was facing the wall when it happened. My god did it happen. Diarrhea. Explosive. Shit cascaded from my ass like rain from the heavens. It seemed like an eternity of poop splashing up against the walls of the stall and all over the toilet. I had crapped so hard that a small toilet shaped silhouette could be seen on the wall. Toilet paper could not clean this mess, and, worse, I thought, it was going to come again. I could feel the second wave building up, but no way was I putting my relatively clean cheeks on that self-created cesspool. I did what any of us would have done, I scooted over, pants around my ankles, on to the next stall. I sat down on this pristine toilet and looked at sad brown lumpy piles of shit under the stall door.

I commenced wiping as I said a quick word of thanks to my Lord and Savior for being a two-stall latrine. It was at this time Pistols came in. I knew it was him because I heard the trailer door open then an immediate, "WHAT THE FUCK??????"

"I know," I replied, "saw that when I came in here. Luckily, this stall was clean." I finished my business, washed my hands, and walked away. Pistols, whom at first I thought was waiting for the cleaner toilet but turned out to be awestruck, just stared in disbelief. He proceeded to drag everyone in the squad over to the bathroom so they could marvel at the wonders of my incognito masterpiece. Now seemingly gallons of shit lighter, I returned to cleaning my weapon.

Years later, I had met up with Pistols, and we were talking about Afghanistan. Somehow, the conversation drifted to things we have had to use to wipe our asses down range. Socks, shirts, underwear. Gauze (him), Four single dollar bills (me). Pistols looked at me and said, “Do you remember that guy that shit the toilet—that was fucked up.”

“Yeah, I remember. Must have been a local national. They never did quite learn how toilets worked.” He laughed. I laughed. My secret safe. My shame hidden.

Lies

On a visit to Bagram on my way home, I perpetrated perhaps my most infamous stunt. There is a saying in the Army that no combat ready unit would pass inspection, and no unit that passed inspection would survive combat. Basically, you can follow all the rules in a book, or you can live, train, and fight. Being stationed way out on a tiny COP had given me a perspective of focusing on the things that mattered to life. Furthermore, those who didn't focus on combat were pussies who probably never fired a gun in anger. It was this attitude that led to the altercation.

Where I was stationed was like the wild west. The ability to shoot straight mattered far more than if you shaved every day. It was perhaps the most and least Army you could ever be. I had been engaged in wearing nothing but flip flops, pt. shorts, a tan tee shirt, and a IOTV (The last being body armor). This is anathema to the modern-day Army that demands the utmost of professionalism at all times. It really divides people into two camps. Those who live outside the wire, where life and death are real concepts witnessed firsthand, and those who live inside the wire (the wire being the concertina wire around every base). Those who lived in relative safety behind their walls of HESCO and concrete operated under a different set of rules than the rest of us. The problem lay in the fact that the real soldiers could still get fucked by not following these arbitrary and sometimes dangerous rules.

I was sleeping in a transient tent a little ways away from the shoppette. This is where soldiers who were just passing through Bagram stayed while waiting for a flight out. It was a pretty easy life those couple of days. Check in at the flight line in the morning and wait till you were called. I spent most of my time reading books or watching bootleg movies on my laptop. It was still too hot out to want to spend any time outdoors. This made dawn and dusk the ideal time to go out and handle your business for the day. Shit, shower, shave, or chow. Most got done in these middle hours. On what would end up being my last day, I was walking to the store when I was stopped. A young, brand-new lieutenant yelled out, "Halt, soldier." Now, as a specialist of some time and experience, I knew my name wasn't Soldier, so I kept walking. "Hey, you," was yelled out again, this time more insistent. I kept my head down and carried on, as my name is not “You" either. Responding to things like these is a good way to find yourself volunteered for all sorts of extra duties. Much to my dismay, the Lt. chased me down. "Why didn't you stop?"

"Sorry, sir, didn't realize you were talking to me."

"Well, you need to be wearing a pt. belt at night so vehicles can see you." Now my head exploded. Are you fucking kidding me? What sort of stupid fucking dipshit would put on a highly reflective piece of clothing in an area with snipers and mortars? Where I was stationed, this sort of thing would get you shot. I stood there dumbfounded as I tried to comprehend and formulate a reply. Before my tongue could untie itself, he continued.

"Why aren't you saluting me? I am an officer. You need to afford me my due respect."

"Welcome to a combat zone, lieutenant, here, doing stupid things like wearing pt. belts makes it easier for the enemy to bracket mortars. The only time you should ever salute someone is if you want them shot by enemy snipers. If you have a fucking problem with that, my name is Sgt Murr with the 18th MP brigade. Till then, shut your cock holster." With that, I sharply saluted and walked away, leaving the lieutenant flabbergasted in my wake.

Now the genius of this makeshift plan was Sgt Murr is a real person in the 18th. So when the inevitable complaint came, the Lt had to explain how he had spoken to a man hundreds of miles away on a seventy-two hour combat op. I wasn't there for that conversation, oh but how I wish that I was.

Heaven

Dearest reader, by now, you have shown me your indomitable will. You have stuck with me through bad times, worse times, and times that were just shit. Even though we may be separated by time and space, we share a connection. To this end, I want to share with you some of my special times in a very special place.

As odd as it might sound, my favorite place in the whole world is the entry control point of combat outpost Herrera. It is here that every night, two different soldiers spend the night staying awake to watch over the others. Guard duty is a long and tedious task. In order to remain vigilant, it is common practice to talk to your fellow soldier. The things we have shared whilst trying to stay awake. Our hopes, dreams, and pasts all laid open and willing. My friendships may have been forged in the fires of battle, but they were quenched in the late-night ramblings of scared children playing at war.

It was here that I met Sgt. Clue. A father of two who was just looking forward to taking his kids to Disneyland. An experience he'd never had. He was going to get out of the army and go to school on the GI bill. Life as a cav scout was okay, it just wasn't for him. He had big plans—he was going places. He was to be a large animal veterinarian. His father had owned a ranch when he was young. Not only did he develop a love for big animals, he learned the value that he could provide as a vet. Clean living in a small ranch house under the Texas sun. Walking outside and enjoying your coffee on the porch. Far enough away from neighbors that all you can see is your land, but close enough that you could help, or get help in turn.

Yes sir. Sgt. Clue had it all figured out. Had. Was. Past tense. Two days later, just twelve days before he was scheduled to leave the country, he died. A routine patrol. I was told the brakes failed on an MRAP, and he ended up getting hit, smashed between two vehicles. I was told it was quick.

I am thankful for the time I got to spend with him. I never met him before, and I will never meet him again. Yet, in the span of eight hours, I can say with certainty that he knew me, and I knew him. Not the causal relationship that passed for friendship at home. But rather, a true, deep knowledge and understanding of who we were. This was one of the first deaths that I had faced. What struck me was the sheer banality of it all. Who survives the worst war has to throw at him only to die in essentially a car accident? I don't think I was prepared for that. I don't know if you can prepare for that.

Face

Me and Pistols, having been on the same squad, spent most of the deployment together. Out of everyone in the world, I have seen the most shit and have the most shared experiences with him. Pistols is a bit of a character. I am unsure how to write him without overshadowing myself. He is an avid practical joker with the type of skewed humor that always seems to end with someone being pushed too far. I was about to write never have I come closer to killing someone. I suppose that is not true. I have killed someone. I have killed four someones. But neither here nor there. Pistols, we liked to refer to him as half terrorist. He was Pakistani and Italian. His favorite joke to play was to don a fake accent and pretend to be a local national. Once, on a long mission, this particular joke came to haunt me.

The most important thing on any mission we do downrange is security. In a slight tangent, let's explain the term down range. A range is an area where you can shoot targets with firearms. I suppose you could say bow and arrows as well, but that is not important at this juncture. Down range is the place where the targets are. Where the bullets fly. Thus, to be downrange means to be in a combat zone. As we were in Afghanistan, the bullets you want to fly are the ones from your gun as opposed to the enemy. So, no matter where we were, at least one person was on the lookout for the enemy.

Tangent number two. I make reference to the enemy. During my deployment, insurgents was the common nomenclature. Before that, terrorists. I would say it is a matter of good guys versus the bad guys. While I am positive that they are bad guys, I can no longer say for certain that I myself am a good guy. For simplicity sake, I reduced the conflict to its base components. Us vs them. Merriam Webster dictionary lists the definition of enemy as a person who is actively opposed or hostile to someone or something. In this case, they were hostile toward me and my goals of not dying. So, if I refer to them as the enemy, you now know why.

We were camping out under the stars. Pleasant night out. It was probably in the low seventies. I could put this in Celsius as the majority of the civilized world does, but I won't. Suffice to say, it was not too hot, not too cold. The embers of a campfire glowed softly against the night. The only sounds were the soft metallic clicking of a traversing turret and the gentle rustling of trees in the breeze. My alarm woke me up. It was 0200 hours, and it was my turn to pull overwatch. I yawned awake as I stretched myself out. Despite the abruptness of the alarm, I was well rested. One of those perfect nights in, at least for the moment, an idyllic locale. The truck was parked up a small hill. I checked my weapons. First, I relieved myself with a long, well deserved piss, then headed up to relieve Spc. Chile from guard duty.

I strapped on my armor and headed into the truck. Chile was in the turret. I could only see his legs, his head was poking out the top, and he couldn't see me. Or hear me as I called his name. "Chile, Chile!" I called out. I tapped his leg to make sure he was not asleep. Then I saw the bottom of a size ten boot. It slammed me in the face. I tasted blood. My eyes instantly welled up with tears. I was positive my nose was broken.

"Get the fuck out of the truck!" Chile screamed. Now I didn't know what the fuck was going on, but I knew I had just been kicked in the face, and this would not stand. I pulled out my pistol and turned it around. Grabbing it by the barrel, I struck back. Accentuating every blow as I screamed back, one word at a time.

"WHAT. THE. FUCK. I WAS. JUST. TRYING. TO. TAKE OVER. GUARD DUTY. YOU. FUCKING. ASSHOLE!"

By this time, the fracas had woken up several members of the squad, and they raced to the truck to see what the matter was, running up in a state of half undress, every last one armed to the teeth and ready for battle. I once read, 'sleep softly in your beds tonight for rough men stand ready to do violence on your behalf for those that do you harm.' My squad embodied that sentiment that night. Ssgt. Rod stopped the attack. He pulled us both down out of the truck.

Chile had thought I was a local national. He'd thought this because thirty minutes prior to my shift change, Pistols had decided it would be funny to feel up Chile's legs while pretending he was a local national interested in sex. I of course knew none of this. When I had touched the side of his leg, he had assumed I was the Afghan that Pistols had pretended to be.

As he explained the story, everyone just devolved into fits of laughter. The following day, I had to report to the captain in charge of COP Herrera and explain to him the tread shaped bruising around my black eye. The only thing, it seems, that is faster than the speed of light, is the speed of a funny bit of gossip. By the end of the day, every single person on the COP had come on by to point and laugh. Surely, Pistols had struck a devastating, if somewhat unintentional, blow in the soon to be all-out prank war.

Timeouts

Intermingled with the missions and ECP or KP or the myriad of other little duties they find to help occupy your time downrange, I would on occasion find myself with some time off. This is kinda shit, because if I wasn't doing a duty, for sure, members of my squad would be. So a weird juxtaposition occurs where your time off tends to be the loneliest of your time in Afghanistan.

That said, you could often occupy your time by watching illegally pirated movies—either ones you downloaded from home, or ones you bought at the local bazaar—going to the

MWR tent in the vain hope that one of your friends or family members was available, knowing the eight and a half to eleven and a half hour time difference made this unlikely. Or just bullshitting around on whatever games you happened to bring with you. For me, I played a lot of Diablo 2 and watched a lot of movies. I had tried reading, but paperback books took up a lot of space and were not really functional in a combat zone.

I read the bible cover to cover twice during this time, perhaps in an attempt to make sense of an otherwise senseless environment. I gained nothing. No deeper understanding, no greater purpose. I think, if anything, it reinforced the chaos that seemed to exist all around me.

Personally, this meant that my free time was probably my most hated time in country. It was a time when you were often forced to face the gravity of the situation. This was when you remembered your wife was three thousand miles away. When you wondered if she's as faithful as her letters implied or if some douche from work had convinced her that that proximity meant intimacy. I counted no less than six dear John letters others had received that I witnessed personally. As in, dear John, I'm banging the neighbor. I lived in constant dread of receiving one from my wife.

This was also the time you missed your family. Inevitably, they were facing some problems that you were unable to help with. You might as well have been on the moon for all you would be able to do. Just a plane ride, in actuality, but worlds apart in practicality. Conversation was limited in both frequency and duration. How do you tell your mother that you killed someone today? How do you tell your daddy that you held a friend's hand as he passed from this world? These are not hypotheticals—if you know, please tell me.

Incoming

There are few things in this world that I detest more than incoming mortar fire. Where I was located, this was a favorite tactic and tool of the enemy. What struck me was always the seemingly sheer indiscriminate destruction of it all. It wasn't a weapon fired in anger, or at least not the hot anger that burns in warriors, but rather a calm, calculated tool of destruction. Mortars that were fired were just as apt to hit us as to hit the locals on or near our base. They were fired often and irregularly. Morning, noon, or night.

I have heard the sound described as a whistle or a hum. The truth is, if you had heard the sounds of mortars overhead, you would know it. You would get the tightness in your gut. You would feel the fear tingle your spine. Not fear for yourself, but fear for others. It has been my experience that if you hear the mortar, you are fine. It is passing overhead somewhere. If you just hear an explosion, run. You are danger close. No, your greatest fear from mortars (or at least mine) was that they would take someone dear to you. Like an ardent thief in the night, with a light and a sound—a best friend gone.

In many things, you expect some semblance of fair play. I shoot at people who shoot at me. Mortars don't have that. Devoid of rhyme or reason, they just come and take. I could describe for you in great detail, the acrid smoke. The silence afterward, broken only by the screams of the injured. The smells, the tastes, the devastation wrought by pockets of things being erased. But I won't. Suffice to say, you either know what I am talking about or you don't.

I was mortared the very first night I was in country. On Bagram airfield staying in transient tents with our whole company. Some two hundred plus individuals, few with any idea what was happening. First, we heard the whine. Then we heard the explosion. Then sirens. Chaos ensued. This was not planned for. This was not explained. There was no battle plan for this enemy course of action. Some people threw on gear, although this varied in both type and amount. Most grabbed weapons.

Spc. Rack, a desert war veteran, donned full MOPP gear. This is equivalent to him wearing a full hazmat suit. Thank god for sergeants. Where there was chaos, they created order. People made their way to the concrete bunker. I assure you, esteemed reader, that this is not a bunker like you are thinking of. It is a cramped square tube. Too short to stand in. Just wide enough that you could sit one person on either side if they interlocked or alternated knees. It was here that you spend not only the time you are being mortared but the foreseeable future afterward until an all clear was called. This has ranged in my experience from fifteen minutes to eight hours.

Flashing back on the soldiers that we played at or the sardines which we were, I have never really been more alone. Surrounded by my fellows, each of us faced our first real brush of our mortality as we waited for the one that would fall and take us away from all of this. At the time, I was probably in physical contact with no less than five separate people, and yet I was all by myself, isolated in the desert of my fears.

Yet again, it was the sergeants who restored order. People played bunker musical chairs as we got into proper units and got accountability. If you only take away one thing from reading this, let it be the importance of sergeants. A sergeant is by definition a bastion of order and professionalism. They control the battlefield in a way that no officer ever could. Moreover, the majority of missions that have seen successes, did not happen because some two-bit pansy ass officer said so, they happened because a tough as nails beacon of warrior spirit sergeant made it so. Do not let movies and books fool you. The men on the ground, outside the wire, have a tendency to be enlisted. The men looking at maps inside the base, drinking coffee, tend to be officers.

For sure, this might not apply to special forces, or some variant thereof. I am also sure that there are good officers who look out for their troops. I believe in them the same way that I believe in sasquatch. Sure, they might exist, but I sure as shit never seen one. It has been my experience that the best you can hope for in an officer is that they don't get in your way too much.

I digress. The point of this section is to talk about mortars. I have faced this type of attack many times during my deployment. I am sure you could count up the total number of times I've been attacked this way, but I didn't, so to me they are countless. My deployment had me move around a bit. The vast majority of my time, I was in Combat Outpost Herrera. Then I was moved to Forward Operating Base Gardez. Finally, I spent part of my last leg of the deployment at Combat Outpost Wilderness.

By the time I had hit COP Wilderness, mortar attacks were old hat. It should be noted that I was sent there singly. I was certified on a weapon system that another squad was not, so I was to go down and help teach the system. At this time, I was the only person to my knowledge to have actually used the system in combat. At least in my platoon. I was assigned to a team with who would later become one of my life-long friends. Balto. Unfortunately, the last member and person in charge of the team was, in technical terms, a douche.

Sgt. Zimmerman; note the Sgt. Even if the man was trash, you need to respect the rank. Now this particular waste of oxygen did not like me, and I did not like him. He was a reclass from infantry. While I was sure that this was true, there was almost nothing else I could be sure of. The man was a liar. Not only in his words, but his very actions betrayed him. I am sure you have met the type. A paper tiger, pretending he was dangerous.

I learned this information from the very first night I was with him. We went to chow as a team. Midway through the line, the mortar siren went off. This brave soldier, this stalwart mountain of a man, threw his tray in the air, grabbed Balto by the back of his ACU jacket and dragged him out the door in a running stumble into the concrete bunker. By the way, I stress, literally, threw the tray in the air. Not dropped it, not set it down. But chucked a full lunch tray straight up. I have been here before. Well, not here, here. All alone in an unfamiliar base with explosives raining down from the sky. But rather, under attack. If experience had taught me one thing, it was to take control over your situation in any way that you could. So, I brought my food with me to the bunker.

For the life of me, I could not tell you where the cooks, or for that matter anyone else ended up. All I knew was that it was just the three of us in that particular bunker at that particular time. I made it to the bunker maybe fifteen seconds after them. It might have been thirty on the long end. In part, because I wasn't running in a blind panic, in part because I didn't know the base that well, and in some small part because I was carrying a tray of food. So, to the sounds of explosions and sirens, I ate. I offered some to my compatriots, but they were too rattled to accept. In my great wisdom, I realized what was old hat to me, was probably a really rather real experience to them.

I should say that after multiple life or death experiences, sometimes when the mood is right, you just don't care. If it is your time to go, so be it. It should be noted that this only occurs till someone gets shot. Then you remember the stakes. But for a moment, you honestly have little to no concept of your mortality. Live, die, it's just a game. This moment was one of those rare confluences for me. Everything had merged together in a perfect storm of me not giving a shit. If I were to die, at least I wouldn't be hungry.

After a while, the explosions stopped. Later, the sirens stopped. I cannot tell you the exact time, but I imagine it would be about the time it takes an adult male to leisurely enjoy a chicken cordon bleu with green beans, mashed potatoes, and pop tarts. I am sad to report that in my rush to the bunker, I neglected to bring a drink. More than any other feeling, all I remember of the bunker was feeling parched. Apparently, it took this long for the old team lead to grow a pair.

His first words "I can't believe you grabbed your food. What sort of fucking idiot grabs food? You're just going to sit here and eat it while there are fucking bombs going off outside?"

He went on, but, honestly, I wasn't really listening. He wanted me to stand at parade rest, in a bunker that wasn't tall enough to stand, I refused. He then wanted me to do pushups on the gravel while under arms, I refused. I was then told that I would be brought up on charges. I am unfit to be a soldier. “Well, shit,” I said, “I can't wait to hear you explain to the captain how you left a soldier brand new to the base in the chow hall, while you ran away.” If he was half as hard as the look he gave me after that, I would have been in trouble. But he wasn't. He continued to yell until the mortars started to fall again. We both sat down on opposite ends of the bunker. Me ignoring him and him doing whatever the fuck he was doing. Don't ask me, I clearly just said I was ignoring him.

Now, as I have said previously, the Army has taught me to take control of my situation the best that I can. The majority of my deployment seemed to be hours of soul crushing monotony punctuated by brief violent interludes. A lot of waiting around until something happened. Almost as important as my sidearm, was my Game Boy. It really helped maintain my sanity, relatively speaking, I suppose, to have an escape with me wherever I went. It spent most of my deployment in my hands or in my pocket. This, obviously, was the perfect time to play. The dick at the other end saw me sit down and enjoy my brief reprieve from the insanity of life in Afghanistan and said nothing. Eventually the all clear was given, we went to our respective rooms and went to bed.

In my ignorance, I thought that would be it. The following morning, I was woken up early with a demand to meet with the First Sergeant and Captain. I was being given a counseling statement (kind of like a work review), the first step in charging me with dereliction of duty. After it was read to me that I had failed in my duties as a soldier, I was asked if I understood. I said no. “What duties did I fail?” I asked.

“You were playing Game Boy on guard. If you don't see how that fails to meet the standard, I will personally kick you out of my Army,” the First Sergeant replied.

“First Sergeant,” I said cautiously, you could bet your ass I was in parade rest here. Talking to a top was liable to get you in all sorts of trouble. “I have not been on guard duty. I just got to base yesterday.”

“Go get your goddamn team leader here,” he said. This time, it was a flight for my life. As I tore out of the building, he yelled at my back. “He should be here fucking yesterday.” I redoubled my efforts. Top was the real deal. A true Sergeant. One who could move heaven and earth to save a soldier. Then rip out that same soldier's fucking soul when he stepped out of line.

Sgt. Zimmerman reported. The First Sergeant asked him to explain how I was on guard duty. The English language lacks the words for me to explain how he asked. Rest assured, it was more a demand then an askance and more colorful than a goddamn gay pride parade. Upon hearing the now correct if incomplete story, he slowly and carefully spoke through his teeth. “You are trying to hem up a good soldier because he played games when there was nothing else to do.” He reached across and tore the US Army tag off his ACUs. “You don’t deserve to wear this. Now get the fuck out of my sight before I take it off for real,” tossing his tag back at him, as Sgt. Asswipe bid a hasty retreat.

This whole time, I was silent. Stunned, waiting in the room for something to happen. Afraid to leave or say anything. He motioned for me to take a seat across from his desk. Then he sat down beside me as opposed to behind his desk. “Son,” he said. “You can and should be in a heap of trouble. Disrespect to a noncommissioned officer is punishable under UCMJ. Your team lead could have you up on that. Fortunately, or unfortunately, that's not what he decided to do. He accused you of doing something a whole lot worse. Understand that if he didn't overreach, I would be taking your rank and putting you to work filling sandbags. Make no mistake, you fucked up here.” I think I tried to speak here, but no words came out, and he motioned for me to be silent anyway. “In this world, you will have to work with and for people you cannot stand. Don't ever let them take your professionalism, don't ever let them stop you from accomplishing mission. Control your actions. Now get out of here and think on what I told you."

"Yes, First Sergeant. Thank you, First Sergeant," I said. Then I left.

Headcase

Sometimes when things aren't going my way, I retreat to a happier time and place in my head. Afghanistan 2009. This was a place where everyone and everything made sense. I knew my role, my place, my purpose. It was a simple time where you were told what to wear, where to eat, and what to do. I miss those simple times where you could tell someone's rank by looking at their uniform, knowing they can do the same to you. The patches on their arm tell you where they are from, and that American flag showed me all of us were on the same team. By knowing their role, I knew mine. A cog in the military industrial war complex. The upside to being a cog in the machine is a cog is useful. A cog has a place. A cog has a purpose, and, therefore, value.

Contrast that with my time outside the military. No mission is set before you. You will not find a task, condition, and standards to throw your kid a birthday party. You will not have a warning order that your wife needs you to fix the dishwasher. Furthermore, no one seems to know their place. The outside world is chaos as each man acts a king in his own right, not following rules or regulations. Doing nothing for the betterment of mankind or the advancement of the mission. People stumble around aimlessly, not knowing their purpose or direction. Often bumping into me, knocking me off my course, making me wish for Afghanistan.

What the fuck are feelings and why should I care if you have them? Why is it my job to ensure I don't offend you? Why can't people just not be offended and do their jobs? My life post Army has shown me that civilians in general are soft. All need to be handled with the utmost care. Lord help us all if I say what is really on my mind. So, I find myself often in a unique position where I have to lie everyday about who I am and how I feel. In a weird way, this has me empathizing with those people who haven't come out of the closet so to speak. It is terrible to have to lie about who you are and how you feel.

On the other hand, I am a pragmatist. A closeted homosexual might be met with scorn or acceptance on announcing to the world who they are when coming out. A veteran with PTSD is much more likely to get locked up or medicated out of his mind. Better I suffer alone free, then suffer at the hands of some VA doctor who barely passed med school passing me drugs once a month.

Leftover

It has been said, my honored reader, that time and tide wait for no man. As we are not exempt from this rule, so too we must press onward to the inevitable. Like grains of sand slipping down the hourglass, we are pulled in ways that we cannot fight. Steel yourself, for the road ahead is rough and full of perils. Once more unto the breach, dear reader, once more. Lest we close the wall up with our dead.

Now that your drama is satisfied and your curiosity unsatiated, we can discuss my most prized possession. A red, duo shock controller for the PlayStation. Now, it is important to note that this is not a particularly good controller. In fact, it is downright terrible. The joystick lists to the left, the x button sticks, and there is an empty hole where the R1 button once lay. As long as we are being honest. The controller wasn't even mine by right. It was stolen. I guess it is not what I stole, but who I stole it from. It belonged to a friend from my past. One who lost themselves and their way upon return from our deployment.

When I hold the controller, I remember the shitty hair metal you played all the time. I remember the bad Jean Claude Van Damme movies you made me watch. I remember more than anything the countless hours we played, taking lives on *Call of Duty* or *Battlefield.* When we got home, the only life you took was your own. Suicide. One word with more pain and more hurt than any other I know. Tears stain my keyboard typing this as surely as they will later stain my manuscript reading this. I hold fast to your memory like a drowning man clings to a plank. At 2 AM, I watch videos of us playing around together. A song comes on the radio that you once sang, and I burst into tears. Driving down the highway, and I am thrown into a rage so black that I beat the steering wheel as I scream to no one. I too am drowning. Is this what you felt? Were you all alone amidst the chaos of your thoughts, trapped by a vortex of negative emotions? Tortured by demons of your own design. You were not alone. You had me. All I needed was a sign, a word, and I would have been there. I would have flown on the wings of Angel's or raced on the hounds of hell if you had but asked. Or had I known to ask you. No, you were not alone. You had me, and I had you. Had. There but for the grace of God go I. I have lost a friend but gained a shitty controller.

Hash

I have encountered hash several times during my deployment. None of them left me particularly enamored with the drug. Generally, I hold drug use in low regard. Having been a soldier, and, more than that, a police officer, I usually think those who use drugs have a tendency to represent the lowest dregs of humanity.

One of the first times I encountered the drug was on the roof of the provincial headquarters building in Jaji Afghanistan. Pistols and I were pulling security with a terp, while others were in a meeting down below. We gazed out over the city. It wasn't late, but the sun was setting. An early autumn night. The twinkling of stars just appearing on the horizon made all the brighter by lack of light pollution that would plague most modern countries. The evening prayers had just finished up, so the city was quiet as people readied for bed.

I don't remember what exactly the conversation was, but I imagine it to be a lively game of fuck, marry, kill. As that is how we often spent the time. For those of you who haven't played the game, you are given three people, one to fuck, one to marry, and one to kill. Spirited debate often waged over the merits or demerits of an individual's choices. For example, you might be given Oprah, J-Lo, and Michele Obama. Pistols smoked a cigarette as we gazed out. A little kid entered as we tried to explain the finer points of the game to our terp. The kid walked right over to Pistols and starts jawing away.

"Your lighter," says the terp. "He wants to borrow your lighter." Feeling a bit uneasy, I'm sure, but wanting to see how this played out, Pistols retrieved the lighter and handed it over. Now this kid couldn't have been more than ten years old. Yet he produced a hash pipe and lit up.

"What the fuck!" I said. "You tell him not to do drugs. Tell him that he is too young for that shit. He doesn't need it." The terp looked at me strangely, then I could only assume he complied with my request as he began speaking to the kid. After a few minutes of them talking back and forth, he speaks to me.

"You know the police chief?"

"Yeah, what about him?"

"He is not really his uncle, he just fucks him." With that, silence. I left. Ever the boy scout, I marched down to my LT and demanded we save him. The LT explained the politics of the situation. This was a good chief. Someone sympathetic to our cause. On top of it, what he was doing was not illegal there. Further, the chief had probably saved this boy's life by bringing him off the street. The justification made me sick. I wish that I could tell you that I marched down and killed the police chief then and there, but I didn't.

I once read for evil to triumph all it requires is for good men to do nothing. Evil won that day. Perhaps one of the biggest regrets in my life. I can tell you that upon egress, I threw up. As if my body was physically rejecting my choice. I see the boy often. Always at night. Always asking why I didn't save him. His eyes plead with me, even as they haunt my dreams.

Depending on how you look at things, the next time I encountered hash down range was either less dramatic or more dramatic. If the boy gave me insight into the reasons why, my next encounter instilled a hatred that ran deep.

We were coming back from a seventy-two-hour op. Hot, tired, dusty—we slowly made our way down what passed for a highway. I was in the lead truck. Gunner. With me, as always, our driver Chile and our squad leader Rod. Today, we were joined by our medic, affectionately known as doc. It was the day that I found out doc had a problem. He was caught doing hash out of the barrel of his 9mm pistol.

Because the only applicable law in county seemed to be Murphy's law, I saw a military aged male flag down the car in front of us. I felt uneasy. I rotated with him as we drove past. Luckily, we were a short convoy that day. Just three trucks. I saw him flag down the civilian cars after us.

I called over the mic "all stop." The level of discipline on the squad was such that all stopped, without hesitation or question. I explained what I saw to Rod. He listened. I loved him for this more than anything. Rather than push forward into an ambush, we broke for lunch.

During the break, we interviewed locals. Air support was inbound. Time to go step on a trap. In what might not have been the moral answer, Rod littered the inside of our convoy with civilians. Now it looked like civie, Army, civie, civie, Army, civie, Army.

The helicopter roared overhead as we made our way through the checkpoint. My hands gripped tight on my 240b. I scanned the distance, searching for the enemy that I knew watched my every move. The air smelled of stale sweat and fear.

"Stay frosty, jokers," a call came over the comms. "We will see you on the other side."

Rod switched to internal comms reserved for just our truck and started running down the list. "Head on a swivel up there, preacher man. I am counting on you to be our eyes." He went on to talk with our driver, then verified comms with not only the other trucks, but the nearest base, and our air support as well.

We approached a narrow pass, if we were to be ambushed, this was where it would happen. "Everyone be chill. Don't worry, if you get shot, doc is right here to patch you up. In no way will getting shot excuse you from gate guard duty tonight." I didn't know if this was an attempt at gallows humor or reassurance.

At mention of doc, I looked below me into the truck. I saw this motherfucker giggling like an 8th grade schoolgirl. He looks up at me. The red eyes and his far away gaze helped clue me in. We may have been a couple of thousand feet above sea level, but doc was higher still. He had used the time we were eating and conducting interviews to get baked out of his goddamn mind.

The most telegraphed ambush I had ever been in, and we were going in for all intents and purposes without medical support. Before this, I might have hated drugs. This was the day that I learned to hate the user.

I don't know if it was the delay, the helicopter, or the fact that civilians were in our convoy, but we were not attacked that day. A convoy the following day was not so lucky. We'd rolled out as QRF to that fight. Remote controlled IEDs, RPGs, and small arms fire. The enemy had melted away by the time we showed up. Four dead. First truck was destroyed in the initial explosion. C'est la vie.

Michael

I was in Bagram on the day that Michael Jackson died. We were eating in the DFAC when it came over the news. Prior to the announcement, we'd been arguing the merits of coming back to Afghanistan as a contractor.

See, earlier that morning, we had woken up and lazily made our way through the chow line. Bagram being a bigger base had an omelet station where you could get fresh eggs cooked however you wanted them. A far cry indeed from the industrial use egg compound served to us regularly at Herrera. After we had made our way through the line, the cook joined us at the table with his own meager breakfast. Out of curiosity, we had made conversation as to how one became an American cook in Afghanistan. I don't remember if at this time he was KBR or Fluor. Both being civilian contractors paid to help run the base.

Interestingly enough, he had been both at one time or another. When KBR lost its contract, Fluor had hired a lot of the exact same people in country as it was cheaper and easier than training or shipping new people. For support contracts, this was a relatively benign process, however, this was also commonplace amidst defense contractors. So, as one got in trouble and it passed to the next one, it was the exact same shitty people doing the exact same shitty things, just a new uniform, but I digress.

So as this nameless, faceless, egg cook sat down, we struck up a conversation. He only cooked eggs and only at breakfast. Seven days a week, four hours a shift. For this, he was compensated eighty grand a year. To put this in perspective, I worked on an average of twelve hours a day during my time in Afghanistan. Seven days a week, mostly doing combat patrols or guarding the gate. For this, I took home thirty grand a year. I am no politician, but perhaps if you wanted to reign in government spending, we could cut contractors and return jobs to the soldiers. Who knows? With all that savings, maybe we could increase the wages soldiers earn.

By lunchtime, this was all we were able to think about. We were out putting life and limb on the line while the dude cooking our eggs made almost triple our salary. While perhaps not life changing information, this was my first time experiencing how little America valued its soldiers despite all of the lip service propaganda otherwise. In the middle of this revelation and realization, came the news. Michael Jackson was dead.

Silence fell over the DFAC. While I had no idea the exact amount of people, it would not be an exaggeration to say that over two hundred people went quiet in the span of seconds. Like a cancer, the quiet spread from group to group, till, finally, you could hear the TV. I do not know Michael Jackson's discography. He is not one of my favorite musicians. Like most people, I assume that he probably abused those kids, and yet I stood in shock at his passing.

Literally stood. I got up from the table with nowhere to go and nothing to do. I wasn't the only one. I looked around as battle hardened killers did the same, as if each questioned the other if this was real life. And as quick as it came, the moment was over. The sound returned. The jokes came in fast. How does Michael Jackson know when to go to bed? When the big hand is over the little one. Why did Michael Jackson go to Walmart? He heard boy's pants were half off. And on and on. Jokes about race, about gender, about death, and most common, about pedophiles dominated the room. Oh, how we laughed. Ha, ha, ha, we chortled in rapturous glee. When we got back to base… reality set in, and we chortled no more. In retrospect, I realize what had happened. Soldiers laughing away the pain. Jokes lend themselves to the ridiculousness of the whole situation. It gives purchase on an unreliable surface. At some point, all you can do is laugh. Otherwise you would have to face the facts of your situation. You are on the other side of the planet from everything you have ever cared for, and, despite the indignity and injustice of it all, the world is moving on without you. This perhaps is what they meant when they said you can never go back home.

Counselling

In the Army, a counselling statement is given every so often, and especially when you fuck up. It says words like, “continue to seek higher education,” and “go to boards if you seek promotion.” Or if you got a negative one, it is likely to state the phrase “This is punishable under the Uniform Code of Military Justice.” I guess you could consider these to be like a performance review at a job. They help shape your future as a lower enlisted soldier.

Well, this is my counselling session with you, vaunted reader. This is a chance to come clean. By this time in my story, you should have a pretty good idea of me and who I am. I warn you, in the utmost seriousness, if you do not like what you are reading, you should not continue. Truth and knowledge do not set you free. It binds you and limits your actions. That is not to say it is all doom and gloom, but there are dark times ahead.

If you decide to continue, if you press on, know that I walk this path with you. Every page is a piece of me laid out for exposure. It is hard for me to write this, for I know what lies ahead. Knowing what I know, and knowing where we will end up, it is almost too much to bear. At the time of writing this sentence, it has taken me six months to write this far. I fear to press on because each word drives me closer to our inevitable end.

So, in conclusion, if you wish to be promoted to reader first class, you need to do something in order to set yourself above your peers. Continue to seek a higher education. These cannot just be words on a page to you. Rather, they should be taken as what they really are. Me, counselling you on how to improve yourself. As well as, you, counselling me, on how to live with myself.

Letters

A good part of my deployment was spent writing or waiting on letters from home. Few letters were received. This, I later found out had more to do with changing of bases and shitty mail service then actual amounts of letters written to me. Personally, I wrote an outgoing letter almost every day. Despite this, few correspondences were actually sent. I would pour out my thoughts and feelings on paper, laying bare my very soul to the recipient. Then tear it up or light it on fire. The brain does a funny thing when you begin to worry. My biggest fear became not the fears of war, but the fears of distance. What if I become a burden to those closest to me? What if they worry and fret? If,

God forbid, my end were to come suddenly and violently, should I leave them feeling like I died scared and alone?

For these reasons, my musings were mostly upbeat and inquisitive. I saved every piece of mail sent to me and kept it in the pocket over my heart. This, while a great sentiment, was probably not the most practical of places to store paper as it was often exceedingly hot, causing me to sweat through my clothes. Despite the loss of literally every letter sent to me, I continued to operate in this fashion. Knowing that I carried the writings of my most loved, provided a spiritual armor to combat the growing darkness in me. It was a tangible connection to a world of sanity and reason. This a physical manifestation of civilization. War is a cruel and demanding mistress, and it is far too easy for it to be all consuming in its savagery.

Revenge

At this time, reader of mine, you should be well aware of several key facts. You know all about guard duty, you know about Pistols and the type of person he is. There is just one more thing you need to know before the start of the story. The remaining information lost to you concerns our living arrangements. During this phase of our deployment, we were staying in B-huts. A small building with eight rooms. On opening the front door, you would see a single hallway extending to the rear door with four rooms off either side. The rooms were hewn in rough lumber and plywood. There was an eight-inch gap under each door. More importantly, there was a two-foot gap between the walls of each room and the ceiling. The doors were locked on the outside via people's individual padlock.

My own bedroom was the same eight by six cell that you would associate with prisons. Except prisons are usually nice. My room gave an air of impermanence about it. A small army cot with a twin-size mattress on top. I made the mistake of sleeping on my mattress the first night I was there. A spring had poked all the way through my sleeping bag to leave a permanent four-inch scar on my elbow. The rough wood could and did often leave its mark on me in the form of various splinters or snagging of clothes. I suppose it said a lot to my situation, or my mentality, that this was what I would call a safe place.

I had hung a hammock across the back wall to sleep on. This was my refuge for bad days. The walls were decorated with the musings of those who came before me. I added my own humble contributions with a black G2 pen. At this time in my life, I would leave such pearls of wisdom as, ‘dress for the whore you want, not the whore you have.’ Or, ‘just once, I wish I could fuck a woman as good as the army has fucked me.’

A small wooden shelf adorned one wall. It was here that I put my laptop and my projector. I could play pirated movies and shows that could take up the whole wall. I am sure that most of you have seen porn at some time in your life but let me tell you, it is something else entirely when it is life sized.

That was it. One shelf, an unused cot and mattress, and a hammock was my whole room. I sat my gear on the bed and my electronics on the shelf. Everything else was kept in my duffel or my footlocker.

Pistols had well and truly pissed everyone off at this point. His jokes always seem to go too far, or when we were too tired. It was exhausting to be around a person who was always on. Thus, like the emperor in Star Wars, it was time to strike back. Pistols had guard duty. His shift ended at 0300 hours. At 0230 hours, my alarm went off. Tonight, the mission required stealth. I quietly stripped down to don my armor of the night. Not the bullet resistant iba or the army combat helmet—rather, a skin-tight, black suit originally meant as a set of thermal underwear, with the addition of a black ski mask and black gloves, it was the attire of a ninja.

The polypro ninja, as it is affectionately known, is a persona who all soldiers are free to adopt during deployment. This battle form gives you insane powers of stealth and is best used to exact sweet, sweet revenge. It can also be used to cause all sorts of mischief. The polypro ninja is perhaps the single greatest warrior in the United States Army. He moves about from person to person or from need to need. Sometimes he works alone, sometimes he is a whole squad, stealing guideons or painting unit patches in the night. Uncle Sam may be the face of the nation, but the polypro ninja does his wet work. Although I could never fully capture the majesty of this elusive warrior, know that he is the soul of honor. When you take on this identity, you lose sense of self, and gain a sense of mission.

Now properly transformed into this agent of righteousness, I proceeded. Pistols' room was beside mine. His door was locked, the lights were off. Using the skills of a misspent youth, I clambered up and over the wall separating the two rooms. Unfortunately, whether due to diminishing skills or the loss of physicality since my youth, I proceeded to crash the six feet on to the floor. Waking almost every person in the hut up.

Fortunately, they were as fed up with Pistols as I was. After a quick explanation, they agreed to not only stay silent, but help improve the plan. All of my squad split up between the Chile's room and my own, the two rooms adjoining Pistols'. I tucked underneath Pistols' bed. The trap was set. Now we waited.

Pistols unlocked his door. I heard him set his rifle on the hook. I saw his feet plod toward the bed. A heavy thud as his sweat stained armor dropped to the floor. Then, I struck. Like a cobra, my arms shot out from under the bed. I grabbed both ankles and yanked. Violently. As Pistols screamed out, suddenly his room was illuminated. I saw his face as it hit the floor in a tableau of strobing lights. The screams took form as he saw the faces of friends, although not friendly faces.

"ITS 3 O'CLOCK IN THE MORNING, DICK!" For some reason, this, more than any other fact, was stuck in his head. He repeated this several times as the rest of the squad piled in his room. We were not a random mob trying to enforce a collective will. We were trained killers, each and every one of us proficient in weapons and hand to hand combat. Perhaps scarier than this, we were trained in tandem in the art of working together. Each individual working wordlessly, knowing how the others would react. We are one body of vengeance, single in our purpose and united through our actions.

In the army, there exists training called forced cell movement. This happens when a team wants to move a violent prisoner with minimal injury or risk thereof. Every person is assigned a single body part. It is their job to restrain and detain said part. This is what we did to Pistols. Five people simultaneously crashed into his appendages and his head. I threw myself over the torso. He didn't stand a chance. We duct taped him to the door. His struggling body a warning of the power of mob justice. His eyes seething, staring daggers that his arms couldn't throw and speaking hate that his mouth couldn't say. I don't know who cut him down, or when, as I was busy sleeping like a baby. The polypro ninja rested. Mission accomplished.

Suicide

Oh, loathsome reader, sitting in your ivory tower, passing judgment from on high. Who are you to criticize me thus? You who have not lived my struggles, only read them. How can someone with such knowledge have so little understanding? It is the difference between reading about the great wall and standing on it. If you were to ask me how many times I have attempted suicide over the course of that damnable year, I would tell you zero. If I start something, I damn well finish it.

Of course, this doesn’t take into account all of the times I had that loaded pistol in my mouth. Finger on the trigger with tension starting to rise. It takes thirteen pounds of pressure to pull the trigger. I must have gotten up to twelve and a half. Maybe I don’t finish everything, or maybe there was never a real attempt. Do you know, reader, what it is to lose? Do you know what it is to take a life? Do you know what it means to be without friends or family? Or do you just sit there reading my story?

I cannot with any certainty tell you why night after night I found myself staring down the barrel of my gun. Just as I cannot with any certainty tell you why I didn't pull the trigger. Life and death had ceased to mean anything. There was scant difference betwixt the two. I wish I could tell you now, years later, that this has changed. I guess in some small way, it has. Life now means more to me with my wife and son. While I certainly don't seek out death anymore, I don't think I will be afraid if it comes knocking early.

Knife

One of the things we did to pass the time in Gardez was to throw knives. We had drawn a small silhouette of a man on a door at the end of a forty-foot hallway that connected the four rooms of our C hut. The back door was never used, as it was further away from the trucks, the shitter, and the DFAC. You would have to go deliberately out of your way to use this door, thus giving us the perfect throwing range.

Of course, if one heard the steady "thwunk" of sunk knives and the occasional clatter of missed ones, it would behoove you to announce yourself before exiting the room. This would save you from the inevitable knife-thrown-at-you-accident. Over time, our whole squad had become pretty good at slinging steel, and the "thwunks" gradually came to outweigh the sounds of knives skittering on the floor.

The key to throwing a good knife lies in the rotation. You want the knife to rotate end over end in such a way that it presents the blade to the target and not the hilt. The easiest way for us to control the rotation was to mark off the distance. So, by controlling one of the variables every time, we greatly increased our chances of sticking a knife in target. We would stick our knives on a post in the wall at the entrance of our building then chuck em the thirty feet or so to the target. Everyone left their own personal knives there so you got the opportunity to throw all sorts of bladed weaponry. Most of which were not designed for throwing.

This all came screeching to a halt with the addition of PFC Crew. I was huckin' and chuckin' as usual when Crew decided to open the back door. This particular throw was a half serrated ten-inch bowie knife with a solid weight to it and a drop point. The knife made a meaty "Thwunk" as it popped Crew dead in the face. Blood poured down as my heart dropped. *What have I done?* evolved into *Why the fuck did he open the back door*? Seconds seem like hours till I hear him shout, "What the fuck? You fucking fuck! Fuck! Fucking bitch!" The string of obscenities flowed forth like water over Niagara Falls crashing down around me with a mixture of raw hate and an odd relief. In the end, it was my skill at throwing knives that helped Crew. I had timed out the rotation perfectly, so when he was a step or two behind the door, it had given the knife enough time to spin and hit him with the back side of the blade and handle.

After that, we threw no knives. While I am sure other people have been hit in the face with a knife, I am also sure that Crew was now a member of a pretty exclusive club, of those who were hit in the face with a knife and survived.

Pride

Reader. As we dive deeper into the depths of my personage, I can't help but to feel a distance growing betwixt us. I can't help but feel your interest wane and your curiosity satiated. Do you perchance know me by now? Do you have a grasp on my psyche so that I may no longer amuse or shock you? Well, the jokes on you. My own grasp of sanity is strained at best. I write without form or prose, because even I don't know what is coming next. You, reader of mine should not presume to know too much.

It is said that pride goeth before the fall and the haughty spirit before destruction. I cannot speak to the veracity of this. I never seem to face the consequences of my actions. Or perhaps in some cosmic jest, this is the punishment I face. Karmic justice led me to you. I remember with great clarity one such instance in which my arrogance could have cost me everything, or at least a very great deal.

As loathe as I am to write this, it bears repeating. It was hot. The whole goddamn country was always hot. Except on the rare occasions in midwinter. In those special moments, it was goddamn freezing. Below freezing. Impossible to stay warm. But this was not one of those occasions, so of course it was way too hot. Now, this story takes place in a Connex. Think of those metal shipping containers that you see on trains or trucks. Essentially the same thing. When in the middle of a burning hot day, these metal containers act like miniature ovens, baking the gear and, in this case, people inside.

For some reason, the powers that be (read officers that have nothing better to do and no real concept of the task) decided that they wanted one hundred percent accountability of every single round that our company had in its possession. To put things in perspective, I will give you my own personal round count. Forty-five rounds 9mm ammo, eight magazines of thirty 5.56mm ammo, or two hundred and forty rounds. A thousand rounds of .50 caliber ammo, and a thousand rounds of 7.62

ammo. That was mine that I was in charge of. One person amidst two hundred and twenty some odd people. And that was not counting all of the extra ammo we'd brought. Only the base ammo that I was carrying on my personage or in my truck. Needless to say, it was numbered in the hundreds of thousands, if not in the millions, and we were to hand count, every, single, one.

So, there I was, baking in the oven that we called a connex. Counting individual pieces of flesh melting metal. Spirits were not high that day. I had been at this for hours, and my own personal count was somewhere in the high five-digit range. I was hot, I was angry. SFC Rose decided that this was an appropriate time to check in.

Now there are two types of leadership. The type that leads from the front, always taking care of soldiers, this type of leader exemplifies what it means to lead. They are disciplined, professional, and selfless. This type of leader elevates the people around him. You work hard for this leader because you know he is working hard right beside you. SFC Rose was not that type of leader.

In the Army, there is a saying. Rank has its privileges. The concept here is the higher you go up in rank, the less actual work you do, the more benefits you can take advantage of. This saying was Rose's life motto. This round count was enforced on E5 and below. E6 were expected to collect reports and consolidate them. Everyone else was to enjoy a day off from their regular stressors jobs of sitting in a tactical operation center and or answering the radio.

So I was angry, I was armed, I was miserable. Rose walks up with a shit eating grin on his face. “Hey, guys, how's it going?” he said.

Above all, I am a consummate professional. So, I took a deep breath and relaxed. “If you would kindly shut the fuck up and leave me the fuck alone, I could finish this goddamn count and go back to the AC. Sergeant.” Now, for those of you who have never served, this was kind of a big deal. It is the equivalent of your team leader’s manager’s boss. He was flabbergasted. Truly at a loss for words, he turned around and walked away.

The rest of the squad started. Mouths agape, they looked at me in a combination of horror and awe. “You can't say that,” someone said.

Then it dawned, a grim realization of what I had said. “Well, it's done now, so shut your cock holsters and get back to work.”

I think that we all recognized the break from sanity. Little slights seemed to take on a different perspective when you walked around armed and faced life or death scenarios. For sure, I was not the only to suffer this break from reality, I was just the latest. I say break from reality, in truth, I felt break from society would be more accurate. There is a time when you reach the pinnacle of human understanding, in which you realize that the rules and regulations that bind you are just artificial constructs.

You hold within yourself the power to break these chains. Especially downrange. You have a gun and you have used it on another. At a certain point, it doesn't matter. Or maybe it does matter. I don't know. Maybe I am as crazy as the doctors at the VA keep telling me. All I really know is that a lot of people seem to count on me following societal rules, and I am not sure that I am going to. If anything, I feel like I am entering reality while everyone else walks around in a haze.

I am sure that the others in my squad had recognized and empathized with my situation. We worked in silence. After a few more hours, we finished. Unbeknownst to me, one of the greatest powers in the Army was visiting that day. The USAREUR commander, a three-star general. A man who was on a first name basis with the secretary of defense and known by the president of the United States. He was there, and he wanted to speak with the troops.

I stood in the back of the makeshift formation, not wanting to draw the attention or ire of my platoon Sergeant. Rather than the super strict, everybody in line you see in parades or on tv, this was more informal. He gathered everyone around, with the front couple of rows taking a knee. He told us about the importance and impact of the mission we were doing. How we had captured a known IED maker who had claimed more than a few US lives. He also explained the value we provided to every mission by ensuring proper prisoner protocols were followed.

More than anything, he expressed gratitude to the rank and file. He was grateful that each and every one of us was willing to sacrifice for our country, and proud of the work we had done. I am under no illusion that he gave a shit about me. I doubt that he ever remembers my name. But in that moment, so great was his speech, that I would have gladly died for him. What's more, I would gladly kill for him.

I couldn't tell you if we spent minutes or hours there. So enthralled with his speech, I stood mystified. Suddenly, it was over. Before he walked away, SFC Rose asked if he could say a few words. Then, to my mollification, he called me up to the center of the group. *There goes my rank* I thought, mentally resigning myself to forty-five days of half pay and hard labor. This usually meant filling sandbags between missions. I was fucked. Rose spoke, I didn't catch the first part of it, but I picked up with "...and here is a man so dedicated to the cause that he is willing to tell his own Platoon Sergeant to shut the fuck up so he can accomplish mission. While I don't approve of his method, the Army sure could use a lot more men like this. True leaders who get things done." I don't know what else was said or done. I weakly remember the 3-star pressing a coin into my hand, saying I was destined to go far.

To this day, I don't know why SFC Rose said what he did. Was it because he thought I needed a win? Was it because he truly believed in me? Maybe it was simply my turn. Second guessing everything will drive you crazy. In the end, I accepted it at face value. A simple coin with three stars on it now lies in a shadow box on my wall. A point of pride on how I was once awarded for breaking the rules.

Preacher

During my deployment, I had picked up the nickname of Preacher. This was not due to some special divinity on my part. Nor was it my habit of ranting for long periods of time. Rather, a spectacular, running, practical joke. I should preface this by saying I am an ordained minister of the universal life church. That is to say, I paid my money to the internet and got legally recognized as a minister so I could officiate weddings and the like.

Not a real pastor, yet I found myself drawn inexplicably toward religion. I started watching old school pastors. Not the seven hundred club people, but rather the fire and brimstone ones of the deep south. Whether this was a true seeking of information or passing curiosity is up for debate. I became enamored with the idea of faith healing. Specifically, the part where the preacher would lay hands on the sick and they would shoot back. This, combined with my ULC certification naming me a minister was a match made in heaven, forgive me a bad pun.

As we all know, idle hands are the devil's playground. So, it became my favorite pastime to slap the shit out of any person I caught complaining.

“My back hurts.” Wham!

“Demons, let go! Release this poor believers' back muscles and trouble him no more!”

“Ugh. Tired.”

“You got demons in ya. In Jesus’ name, demons begone.” Slap!

The penultimate experience came when my team leader was in an ASV. North had his head sticking out of the top of an ASV in full kit. We had just come back from a mission and were all pretty beat. We had to guide the vehicles around base on foot in order to minimize any accidents that might arise from driving four-ton vehicles in close proximity to buildings, people, and other vehicles. At the end of the drive, as he was parked, he shouted something down to me. I hopped up the front of the vehicle so that he might better understand what I was saying.

Seemingly like a gift, I heard him exclaim, "This gear feels like a goddamn devil squeezing my tits." Well, we know what we do to devils.

"Get behind me, Satan," I yelled. North was confused as he looked about incredulously. He had seen the show and should have known what happened next. Alas, he did not. Whap! Straight to the helmet. North goes down. He goes down hard. Those around burst into applause. Or at least in my memory of the event they did. Fuck you guys, I definitely deserved applause here. Even if it didn't exist in reality. The preacher had saved another life.

Blood

Oh, contemptible reader, I can hear your thoughts. You have shared in the loss, you have laughed in the moments of levity, you have experienced my pride. Where is the blood? Where is the killing? More so than any other subject, this is the one I would avoid. Yet this is the one for which you thirst the most. The disconnect happens because I have done this, and you have not. The first question posed to me upon learning of my veteran status is usually how many people have you killed? In answer to the question you are dying to ask, I would reply four.

You can read this however you choose. If you so deign to judge the radical Islamist terrorists who threatened my life and the lives of those around me, then that is your right. Do not however presume to tell me how I should feel about it. You, reader, disgust me. Those four souls are weights around the ankles of a drowning man. It is this aspect of my history that I hate the most. How can you, most vile, revel in such sin. Political differences aside, I have killed fathers, sons, brothers. Everybody is somebody to somebody. While the brain can justify, the heart feels stained. And so, I scrub on my soul like out damned spot!

To me, this is by far the ugliest part of myself. Most nights, it is not the friends that I have lost, but the enemies I have removed that keep me up. For people to praise you for that in which you most revile is a special type of hell. But here it is, damned reader. Here is at least part of the story. Although, damn you thrice for making me tell it.

It was December 24th, 2009. Our squad had the day off. We celebrated this fact by drinking blue vodka that a church was kind enough to smuggle in via miniature scope bottles. I don't want you to get the wrong idea. Not a single one of us was drunk. A half shot of a low-grade vodka is generally not enough to go on a bender. It was enough however to take the edge off. It removed the sharpness of the pain felt in our backs and knees. It dulled the longing ache in our hearts for missing our families on

Christmas. Most of all, it gave us some semblance of normalcy. God bless whatever devious bastards of John's southern Baptist church in Texas came up with this idea.

We were all together when we got the news. The entire squad hunkered down in a small room, laughing as we watched Rudolph for Christmas. The door burst open. "Grab your gear, boys the 92nd is under fire." At the time, I had no idea of who was in danger, or how. Only that people from my company were facing down enemy fire and needed my help. Typically, it took a half hour to get everyone in a truck and on the road for a mission. That day, everyone was ready in less than five minutes.

I was loaded with the m240b machine gun. A belt fed, gas operated, air cooled, medium sized, machine gun that delivered 7.62mm rounds to target at a rate of 650 rounds per minute. It was loaded onto a CROWS 2 system. Insane accuracy. Zoom. Heat vision. An already devastating weapon system made deadlier by high tech innovation. To both my delight and chagrin, it also meant I would be inside of the truck during the firefight. Our truck could carry eight people, although that day we were but four. Gunner, driver, team leader, and terp.

We were operating as QRF, or quick reaction force. We had reports of at least one American casualty at the Afghan police station in Gardez. With weapons locked and loaded, a convoy of trucks raced to the scene. The PHQ (provincial headquarters, i.e. the police station) was situated on top of a small hill. It was matched however on all sides with small skyscrapers. These were not buildings like you are thinking, rather like a hollow structure of a building. The first floors were filled out, but the top more resembled a parking structure than an actual building. Our squad was hunkered down on the opposite side of the road from the buildings. They were receiving fire from the second story.

Our vehicles whipped down the road, placing ourselves as a bulwark against the stream of fire. Before we even stopped, I returned fire. The purpose of the initial shots not to kill the enemy, but to get their head down to buy my friends a few moments respite. A jihadist came across my screen. A tilt of the wrist, a tightening of the finger, he fell. I saw the muzzle flashes of three or four more weapons. I couldn't find the people behind them.

The call came in for dismount. Our driver and team leader stepped out. Joined by the rest of our dismounts, they prepared for entrance. They moved to the building adjacent to the target one. The call came over the radio for suppressing fire. They were moving in. The steady drum roll of machine gun fire above me was interrupted. Weapon malfunction. I climbed up and out the top hatch. To my right, I saw our dismount squad moving forward. To my left was Pistols, standing over his mk19, hip firing an M4 like Rambo, screaming inaudibly. I saw local nationals fleeing the area. One tripped over concertina wire. Others used him as a human bridge. I found out later he was trampled to death.

Bullets ricocheted off my truck. I hunkered down beside my weapon system and fixed the jam. More bullets flew, carving gouges in the armor beside me. I dove back into the hatch, intent on the ability to return fire. The carrying handle on my IOTV armor catches. I had to remove it by pulling a cord located on my chest. This caused the vest to disassemble itself into pieces around me. I tumbled to the floor. I went to fire. The power cable had disconnected. Multi-million-dollar piece of shit. Of course it fails when you need it most. I took the interpreter's flak jacket, climbed back up, and returned fire free hand.

Explosions rocked the building. I didn't know if it was the stream of m203s launching 40mm grenades into the building, or the Russian style grenades that were set up as booby traps. A national guard special forces squad rolled up. They parked in between our guns and the bad guys. They got out on the wrong side of their vehicles, immediately, one went down, shot. They started firing, mostly at our dismounted squad which had by now taken the second floor. After much yelling and screaming, myself and the other gunners pulled them back to the right side of the line. We give them our comms channel. While "speshul forces" prepared to go in, we got the all clear.

Mission was over, threats were eliminated, captured, or escaped. Within two minutes of the cessation of fire, people were trying to mob the trucks in an effort to collect spent shell casings. Within five minutes, the people and the casings were gone as if the TIC was some sort of dream.

There was no doubt in my mind that special forces in the regular army were some high-speed operators. They do amazing things that I could probably not comprehend. Those guys were a fucking joke. Our dismounted squad brought down three captured prisoners. We rushed them to the nearest base. Two were shot. One of them rode beside me as we rushed back to get him treatment. It was just me and him in the back of the truck. Unfortunately, his injuries were just too severe to make it back. Damn shame. I admit to nothing.

If you, reader, cannot read what is not written, well that's on you. I know the writing here is stiff and stilted. I am phenomenally uncomfortable with this part of my past. Damn you again for making me relive this.

Kill

There is a certain level of detachment I feel from my actions in Afghanistan. I was just a tool in the United States military industrial complex. What use is regret to a hammer? Where is the advantage in a screwdriver filled with doubt? Instead, I remained the dependable shop knife, my skills and instincts honed to a fine edge so my commander might wield me where effective.

I once read there was a study done about a level of disconnect of killing someone through a lens. I cannot vouch for the veracity of the particular study, or even point you to exactly where or what it was. I just remember the glass acts as a physical barrier distancing you from your own actions. There were at least three plates of glass between me and my target. The front lens of the scope on my CROWS. The receiving mirror where it transforms the light into data, and finally, the screen where my firing solution and reticle was displayed. Allowing me to zoom and adjust as my target moved back and forth.

There is a saying in the Army that the only thing a soldier should feel when killing a terrorist is the recoil of the rifle. Because of my weapons system, I didn't even feel that. What do I feel? How can I sleep at night doing what I have done? I feel nothing. Regret nothing. I go to sleep at night on a queen size mattress with a designer down pillow. It is you, oh hateful reader, who should be on trial. How dare you presume to judge me?

Loadout

Although I briefly touched on it in the beginning, it occurs to me, oh forgetful reader, that you might use a bit more formalized approach to our gear. Every soldier in my platoon carried a 9mm Beretta pistol, called, appropriately, the M9. For this, the combat load of ammunition was forty-five rounds. Walking on base, to everywhere but the shower, you were expected to carry at least this weapon loaded with a single fifteen-round magazine.

Additionally, most soldiers carried an M-4 rifle. This, for those of you living under a rock for the last decade, is the platform that you hear so often about on the nightly news as the base platform for assault rifles. The M-4 has a collapsible butt stock and a shorter barrel in comparison to the M-16, making it far better suited to close quarters combat. It fires a 5.56mm round at a rate of over 700 rounds per minute on cyclic. This is unachievable in real life as it is not a belt fed weapon. Our basic combat load for this was two hundred and ten rounds placed in seven thirty-round magazines. It was commonplace, in my squad anyway, to have the last three rounds of a magazine to be tracers so you know when it's time to reload.

Team leaders had an M204 grenade launcher attachment for their M4. This fired several different flavors of grenades. Smoke, high explosive, and high explosive dual purpose being the most common. I know they carried seven individual grenades but could not tell you the exact composition of their loadout as I was not a team leader and am frankly too lazy to google it or email a comrade.

Drivers carried the M249 machine gun in lieu of an M4. This is a belt fed weapon. Their standard combat load was six hundred rounds, carried in three separate 200 round plastic drums. On smaller trips, it was not uncommon to see a driver with a smaller hundred round cloth-based drum, affectionately known as a nutsack. Their weapon platform was heavier by a good deal than the M4, and I imagine most just wanted the relief.

Everyone carried a knife of some sort, this was primarily used to open tough MRE packages, but, as a weapon, deserves to be included.

As an MP, we worked in teams of three. One driver, one gunner, one team leader. The gunner is only semi-assigned a crew served weapon. Really, the weapon belonged to the truck. Most of the time, we worked with and on the same vehicles, and as such had the same weapons. However, this was not always the case, and, occasionally, you would have to track down whoever had your truck's weapon before a mission, and most likely chew them out for not properly servicing it (early on in my deployment, I had a jam on a fifty cal during a firefight, it was less than ideal).

Crew served weapons included the M2 fifty caliber machine gun, the Mk19 40mm grenade launching machine gun, the M240B 7.62mm machine gun, and the aforementioned M249 machine gun. Most of these were pintle mounted in a turret, leaving the gunner half in and half out of the truck. The turret usually had half walls, affording the gunner some protection, and an angled plate on the front, known as the chicken plate. CROWS trucks could carry the same weapons but mounted to a robot and a video camera on top of the truck instead of a turret. In these trucks, the gunner sat inside with a joystick and a small monitor. ASVs carried two crew served weapons, and the turret was internal. They had both the M2 and the Mk19. They also afforded the least amount of space and visibility to the gunner. Thank Christ I wasn't an ASV gunner.

This was the mandatory carry for our platoon. It gets a little different in that some chose third party add ons. Like EO tech laser dot sights instead of ACOG scopes. Quick pull magazines were also popular. Seems like everyone had their own version of sling or holster as well. The rule here was practicality and function over uniformity. If you could fire the weapon, you could carry it and ammunition in any manner you saw fit. This is why soldiers never look the same kitted out. Flashlights and forward grips were commonplace additions.

As the squad leader's gunner, I also carried the majority of our demolitions. Five hand fragmentation grenades, two smoke grenades (one green, one red) a flare, and a SMAW bunker buster (think bazooka, only much more advanced). Others carried hand thrown grenades as well, but it was a lot less ordered and more; if you want to have a grenade, you can have one, type thing.

We all had the same type of body armor, the IOTV. We all carried a first aid kit. The first aid kit had a tourniquet, gauze, tape, nasopharyngeal, rescue breath mask, abdominal pad, and muslin dressing in it. Most people brought a small backpack called a go bag or assault bag to carry MREs and assorted other knick knacks or explosives or ammunition.

Angel

I don't really know how I feel about you, reader. You are both my priest taking confession and my condemner passing judgment. Beyond that sentiment is a deeper issue of not understanding myself. You serve as a mirror for my own insecurities. In you, I see everything that is wrong with society. Yet, I also see the hope for the future. You are simultaneously damnation and salvation. Forgive me a touch of the introspective.

I have an Uncle, J. E. Without going into too much detail, it is sufficient to say he was somewhat of a father figure to me. Not that he played a large role in my life, rather he was part of a group of men who I decided I wanted to be like when I grew up. My own father was not in the picture, so I got my ideas of manhood based on an amalgam of men I thought were doing it right. Humphrey Bogart in Casablanca, among them. From J.E. I take my stoicism and kindness. He was more than a great man—he was a good man.

Sgt Moron. He has a real name that I am sure is not actually moron. Other names I have changed for privacy or other reasons. His name honestly just can't be bothered to remember. Downrange, we referred to him as Moron. In this aspect, it is probably the first real name I have given you besides my own.

Ssgt. Rod was a good sergeant. He looked out for the squad and was genuinely invested in our success. Unfortunately, he got to go on leave. Rather than remain a cohesive unit and have a team leader in our squad act as squad leader until his return, we got Moron. Moron didn't know us or care to know us. It is soldiers like Moron who made the charge of the light brigade an immortal poem instead of a successful military advance. (For those unfamiliar with the poem, it covers the idiotic advance into enemy artillery ordered by an incompetent officer. The best line being "Theirs is not to question why, theirs is but to do and die." In this same way, we were expected to execute orders.)

Our mission was to search a qalat, or village, a few kilometers outside of base. We did this in the middle of the day. A few other squads were setting cordon. This meant they were in a circle around the village. No one got in or out without our say so. Our squad was to go in and search. Rather than drive our trucks in on the road, Sgt. Moron decided on a dismount entrance. Rather than walk on or alongside the aforementioned road, Sgt. Moron decided on walking around the back of the village through a field. A minefield. This knowledge was not gained through the benefit of hindsight. Rather, I expertly gleaned it from the fence around the field with the little red triangle signs on it. Signs with a picture of an explosion. Signs that our interpreter assured me meant mines. This was to be our entrance. They would never see us coming, though a wide-open field lacking in cover and concealment...

But wait! There's more! Without going into too much into detail, there are two basic military formations you should know. Line, and column. A column is a single file line, much like you were forced to stand in grade school. The only difference being we left about five meters in between each person. A line formation is red rover red rover. Guess which one Sgt Moron wanted to do. Through a known minefield. Now, being the gunner in the squad leaders squad let me have access to leadership I might not have otherwise had. In this case, it meant I was carrying the radio.

After Sgt. Moron explained to us how we were crossing the minefield. I took the time to carefully explain to him that he was an idiot. When that got me nowhere, I took the time to radio and explain to our Lt. that for unknown reasons Sgt. Moron was trying to get the majority of our squad killed. The results were a mixed bag. As the highest ranking on the mission, Sgt. Moron had ultimate control. However, he would have to explain in detail the way we handled the mission.

Needless to say, I had not gained a lifelong friend. It was determined that we would walk through the minefield. It had the advantage of the element of surprise. As no one would expect it. Even though it was broad daylight, and a literal field with no cover or concealment. We would be walking in a singular column though. An improvement. Because of, and I quote here, “my smart mouth,” I would lead the column to live or die by “my plan.”

Spoiler alert, I lived. (Largely in thanks to a soldier in my platoon who I named after the directions on a compass. While I haven't done so yet, I want to thank him. If you're reading this, killer, you know who you are... thanks for always letting me know which way is up.) Ironically, although possible inches from death on either side, it was not there that I was in danger, it was the town. We arrived at the first compound. It was a compound in the sense that it was a large, square, walled-off area. Like fortress walls. Inside, there were several small buildings. Sgt. Moron informed me that he'd had it with my shit, and I needed to go find a corner and stand in it. Not pull security, mind you. Not help with the searching of buildings. Stand in a fucking corner like I'm in timeout.

On days that I believed in him, I thanked God for Sgt. South. Through intuition or observation, he saw me go to react and intervened. He walked with me to the corner. We stood, the corner betwixt us, and he talked me down. Not easy to do when I was carrying a loaded weapon. I heard J. E. telling me to calm down and take stock of where I was. "A time and a place for everything," a whisper on the wind.

I calmed down. I started to take notice of my surroundings. Between myself and South was a small patch of dirt that was slightly raised. Not unusual in itself, but it was rectangular. I called the terp over. He started yelling.

"Mine. Mine! MINE!"

"Whatever, dude, yours," I say.

"No," says South. "I think he means it is a mine." This hits me like a ton of bricks. We are standing two feet apart.

There is a landmine not only inches from my feet, but inches from South's feet. Directly in between us. Where I would have been standing had South not come over to speak with me. Where I probably would have shuffled over to once he left. EOD comes. They find eight RPG heads underneath double stacked anti-tank mines. All rigged to a small pressure plate.

I got an award or something. I don't remember. All I could think of was how angry I was that day. Later that night back at base, I went to the MWR and called my mom. I didn't tell her about my day. She told me that my uncle had passed away that morning. The angel on my shoulder. Coincidence, maybe. But it would be just like him to spend his first day in the afterlife looking after his kin.

Blind

I have been blind since birth. Not in a literal sense, rather a legal sense. My eyesight lies in the low 700s. What I see at 20 feet away, most others see that level of detail at 700 feet. This was not caught till I was nine years old. I spent the first nine years of my life under the assumption that everyone saw as I did. That things I saw were normal.

When I finally got glasses, it was a revelation. Things once clouded and blurry were now crisp and bright. I found myself staring at trees or flowers. Things that I once accepted as ordinary took on new life as I could truly see them for the first time. I would constantly look at things then remove my glasses and look again.

This is the closest I have come to describing my experience with war. The scales over my eyes have been loosed. I can see life and death in great detail. I am walking around in a world of the blind. In the grand scheme of things, we matter little. The world turns on. Life, love, and happiness are fleeting.

Within three generations, it is likely I will be completely forgotten. That, more than anything, is beautiful. We are but fireworks in the night. A brief flash, then we are gone. I think that it allows me to be free in ways that other people are not. What use is regret to a firecracker? What is the point of self-doubt when you live for such a short time? By accepting my inevitable death, and the lack of meaning in it, I can truly live.

My life is insignificant. My sphere of influence is small. My experience with the human condition is shared across thousands of people. These thoughts have been thought before and will undoubtedly be thought again. Embrace and accept this as fact. It makes you feel like you are not alone.

This clarity is denied to those who blind themselves to the truth. Civilians run around thinking the world revolves around them. When, in reality, we are all cogs in a machine. The army teaches us that it is not bad to be a cog. In fact—each gear is useful to the machine. I guess I'm rambling now.

Ghosts

Oh, vacuous reader, how little do you know. For it is oft written and repeated that men come home from war haunted. I can tell you unequivocally, and without fail, that this is a falsehood. The truth of the matter is ghosts do not exist. My reasoning is as follows.

Afghanistan is a war-torn country. It has been a war-torn area since the beginning. Like the beginning, beginning. I am pretty sure Caine slew Abel in what is now downtown Gardez. It has seen wars from the Persians, the Russians, and now the US led coalition (read US Army and twelve Polish troops). The point is, men have been dying here since forever, and dying hard.

Couple this with the fact opposing forces had people stoned to death for siding with American troops. A mob literally threw rocks at someone till they died. Multiple someones, in fact. The crux of my argument comes down to three main points.

To get ghosts, people need to die. Obviously. Without dead people, who would make up the ghosts. Check. People have been dying at quantity for thousands of years in this area.

People should die in terrible ways in order to maximize the chance of a ghost. I don't know if this is true or not, but it seems to be a recurring theme in ghost stories. I'm relying on the tribal wisdom passed down through spoken word here. Anyway, check. This requirement is overfilled. People have been dying by inches and in droves.

Lastly, a possible graveyard connection. Maybe ghosts are tied to their corpse. I was stationed on a base that had a 300-year-old graveyard smack dab in the middle of it. Plenty of corpses.

The entire time I was in Afghanistan, I had seen not a single ghost. Furthermore, I had not heard any ghost whispers or seen any ghost lights. I have personally examined hundreds of photos that I had taken of my experience and came up with zilch.

"But, Rodney… ghosts are real," you whine. First of all, it's Sergeant, and, no, they are not real. I have spent many a night at the raid tower looking out with heat vision cameras. No phantom forms. No fellow soldiers have ever told me of an experience while we were deployed.

Some ghosts are an imagined threat your mind conjured up to keep you wary of the dark and unknown. Some ghosts are your brain helping you cope with a loss. Good survival mechanisms. In a wartime environment, the threats are real. You do your best to compartmentalize, not to cope. Ghosts are simply a luxury not afforded to soldiers.

Deadfinger

During the winter months, I had accidentally slammed my finger in the back hatch of an ASV. I was more than a little upset, as I did not drive or ride in an ASV. The hydraulics on this particular vehicle were broken. I was retrieving my Game Boy from a friend who borrowed it for a long mission and was told to just grab it from their bag in the back of their truck. I don't know why this makes it so much worse, but, rest assured, it does. Much like Kevin Smith's character Dante in *Clerks*, "I wasn't even supposed to be here today."

I was lucky in the fact that I did not lose my finger. It did, however, look like I was going to lose the nail. It grew this deep shade of purple as it swelled up. It released from the back of my nail bed and flapped open and closed like a car hood, only in reverse. The worse bit was the smell. Something was definitely going on under the nail. I was afraid infection had started to set in.

Crew came to my aid. I had spent the hour soaking my finger in isopropyl alcohol. He grabbed the back of my fingernail with a black Leatherman multipurpose tool. I bit down on a stick wrapped in shoelace. He pulled, and my world ended. To those of you who haven't had your nails pulled out by a pair of pliers, I am not sure that I would be able to accurately describe the sensation. I have had root canals, kidney stones, and have just been plain kicked in the nuts. All paled in comparison to the pain I felt that day. I saw stars form and die in front of me.

The worst part was that I had asked for it. I'd let him do this to me. Granted, there were no medical professionals for god knows how many miles and through god knows how many enemy combatants. All I know is that if you ever think it is a good idea to pull off your nails—don't! I am pleased to report that a new nail grew in. The skin underneath it looked very infected, but was better after a few cleanings, fresh dressing changes, and exposure to the air. Perhaps, if you look closely, you can tell it is of different shape than the others but is not very noticeable. I am sure that if you take stock of your friends and family, someone you know has suffered a similar injury.

What does it all mean? Why, in a book with death and debilitating injuries, would I take the time to cover something so inconsequential? To me, this is just one of the little moments, hurts, and changes that a person goes through over the course of a year. The scar on my elbow from a mattress spring or the multiple wrist surgeries, it is one more thing that my friends and family back home won't recognize. I cannot say if it was the experience of injury or the minor disfigurement that unsettled me, in the end, it was just one of a thousand minor cuts separating me from loved ones and the past I once knew. A physical reminder that time marches on.

Meals

In order to provide you with a better understanding, reader of mine, I have decided to do micro chapters that go into detail about some of the more mundane aspects of my life downrange. This one, oh glorious reader, concerns my daily sustenance.

Mealtime should be split into three parts, really. Hot food on base, cold food off base, and hot food off base. The first of these is generally preferred. The quality and quantity of these were largely dependent on the location and size of the base you were on. These ranged from forward operating bases to combat outposts. The former having multiple dining facilities (or dfacs) with a variety of options. The latter limited to one with set hours.

Hot chow on Bagram stood at the pinnacle of all the food in Afghanistan. Multiple lines multiple options. Freshly made omelets for breakfast and steak and lobster on holidays. Don't get me wrong, it was not as good as say an Outback or an Applebees. But for army chow, it does not get any better. Of all the army meals, my favorite was chicken cordon bleu. I found the exact same in Kroger's in the prepackaged food section. I don't know what it was, but for some reason, it always reminds me of home.

Most of the deployment, I ate Clif Bars taken from the dfac. I would have these with crystal light lemonade packets mixed with the always readily available lukewarm water bottles. I tried with some success to cut weight by eating six to seven meals of 400 calories a day. This to be as cut as possible when returning home to my new wife.

The best thing you could eat in the entire country had to be the bread. Always hot and fresh, it reminded me quite a bit of naan. They served theirs round at about twelve inches in diameter. It was a little doughier perhaps then naan, but boy was it good. I would send the terps out on the market to bring me back ten of them at a time. This served as the basis for most of my meals downrange.

It was important to me at the time to attempt to get into peak physical condition. I had taken to eating several small meals a day in order to maximize my metabolism. This, coupled with hours at the gym, had me returning from Afghanistan to a bunch of clothes that didn't fit.

The Dfac and the veggie omelet MRE, both carried M&Ms, peanut of course had been my favorite. An event later ruined plain M&Ms for me. Myself and Chile would go out of our way to secure packages for the both of us. Before the deployment, I had never really like them, but during, they were pure sex in a paper wrapper. Nostalgia brought home by those little candy-coated chocolates.

The other food, or, more specifically, drink that was worth the trip, the tea. They called it chai, but that is literally just the word for tea there. It tastes nothing like the teas in teavana or any other high-end tea shop I could find. Some of my best memories were of sitting down and sharing tea with the locals. They did not sweeten the tea there the way we do. Rather, you held a bit of rock candy in your mouth while drinking the tea. Whether this was common practice or just something they made up to see what stupid shit we would do has yet to be determined. But, goddamn, it was good. I have spent many years searching, trying to recreate that perfect cup of tea.

Women

Women in combat, and the problems thereof. Ah my intrepid reader, today I would discuss my experience with some of the fairer sex downrange. I could tell you of the fidelity or valor of PFC Maner or PV2 Panda, but I won't. Largely because they were not in my squad, so my firsthand experience with them is limited. Instead, I would speak of those that I did have contact with.

Dookie was the lone female in the squad. As such, certain concessions were made the entire time for her benefit. If we had two tents, she was given one, and the other eleven of us would cram into the second. This privacy, I later found out was put to very good use, as she had slept with no fewer than three members of our squad, and who knows how many outside of our squad.

Dookie also was a vegetarian. While this wouldn't ordinarily bother me, as I only like some foods myself, I found this most irritating. She laid claim to all the vegetarian MREs, which were arguably the best tasting ones. We would have to add a veggie option to all of our meals. Again, this wouldn't and shouldn't bother me. What really made this untenable, however, was the fact that I personally witnessed her eating chicken, pork, and beef in the chow hall when she didn't like the vegetarian option. We had to accommodate her diet based on what she felt like eating as opposed to a strict diet or religious reasons. This abuse of hospitality made me dislike her almost more than any other reason.

On patrol, if she decided her pack was too heavy, someone else would have to carry it for her. Once on patrol, rather than risk a hike down a hill, she'd sat on her ass and scooted down the narrow trail. At the base of the hill, she had discovered she was now covered in goat shit. In what you should now consider a typical Dookie reaction, she had demanded we return to the base and retrieve a fresh pair of pants.

Later in the deployment, she had managed to both hit a wall and get her MRAP stuck in a shit trench. Five other drivers made that turn without issue. We were stuck for hours, awaiting a wrecker from the base to help us. It was during this time I told her she was a terrible driver. Many hours later at the FOB I was brought in to the TOC to discuss my sexist remarks. She had told leadership that I said she was a terrible driver because she was a woman. When in fact I said and meant she was a terrible driver because of her shit driving abilities. While I didn't get in trouble per se, a record was kept on my file with a complaint of gender biased.

We also had a cook deploy with us who prided herself on the fact that she was sleeping with a guy on the base who was in the special forces. This seems a stupid thing to me to take pride in, but whatever floats your boat. Toward the beginning of our deployment, she started having problems with one of her NCOs. She claimed that after a verbal altercation, the NCO in question took out his dick and waved it at her.

The company rushed to her defense. She moved platoons, transferring her away from the offending NCO. The NCO came very close to losing his rank, and in the end, lost his promotion to the next rank. We closed in around her, providing every bit of support we could muster. To think that you deploy to Afghanistan only to be sexually assaulted or harassed. I was proud of our response to this incident.

Within the month, she had problems with another NCO, this one a family man. Naturally, she accused him of getting into an argument, then mid fight, he pulled out and started waving his dick at her. I don't think people ever took her seriously again. I don't know the true story. She might have been suffering from PTSD. She might have been telling the truth both times. While surely, it is not for me to judge, I left that whole situation feeling more than a bit jaded.

Porn

One of the worst things about my deployment was the copious amount of time I had. What can distract you from the horrors you faced in the day or that you know are going to face tomorrow. Family and friends are thousands of miles away, and communication is spotty at best. The answer, of course, thousands of hours of downloaded pornography. It was common practice to carry thumb drives in which you could swap or trade pics and videos. This should have been, but almost never was, done with caution. Not for fear of viruses or the like, rather a bunch of people accidentally traded away homemade versions featuring wives or girlfriends.

I had found the secret to preventing this was compartmentalization of stuff that was not to be traded was kept in a hidden folder on my computer itself. Not mixed with any of the others. As a result of unsafe porn practices, I am sad to say that a bunch of us have seen others in action. Being young men, we have of course approached this in the most mature way possible. By disseminating it widely and critiquing performance in a loud and public manner. We also mercilessly teased the fool who had the misfortune of accidentally sharing bi porn. As far as we were concerned, this was just gay lite.

Tangent. I don't care if you are gay. I really truly do not. Some of the finest men I have ever known are openly gay. However, it was the ultimate insult to call someone gay or a faggot. I think that this isn't because of what you might like to do in the bedroom, it's more the idea that you are hiding it. I respect and admire the men who are brave enough to come out and say that they are into things that the rest of us might not be. To me, those are real men. In closing, I guess it is just a guy thing, no insult intended to those who are, and every insult intended to those who are not. I could go on and on about the subject, but either you understand at this point, or you don't.

Have you ever been so bored that you have watched a porn from start to finish? I don't mean when you are finished, but rather all forty-five minutes of wonderful, terrible action. While I can't speak for my female compatriots, I can assure you that most men watch ten minutes of any given film. Having the kind of time and boredom to watch a porn from start to finish is unhealthy to say the least. The kind of cinematic gems you can find however, make it almost worth it. For instance, in one, this lady had a zit on her posterior. Much to the gentleman actor's chagrin, it popped while mid ride. I saw him wipe it off on her lower back without missing a stroke. The lady none the wiser.

Another time I saw two gentlemen enjoying the company of a lady at the same time. While her mouth was free to kiss, other entrances and egress points on her body were, how would you say—occupied. As the gentleman on bottom finished up, he pulled out his generous Tommyknocker and started knocking on her front door. As you are want to do in this situation, to ensure the pipes are well and truly laid. The only problem was that this wasn't a solo act. Instead of the nice pillowy entrance of a well-managed muff. It was the testicles of gentleman number two. Now ever the consummate professional, number two is trying to cup his balls while number one is whacking away with his package. Probably the most dramatic piece of cinema ever filmed. If you want to know the ending, message me, I'll send you a link.

Because young men strive to make any awkward experience more cringey, it was commonplace to cheer on your fellow soldiers if you heard them playing porn. Shouts of you can do it, and one for the gipper were often heard intermingled amidst the various moans of fake pleasure.

Pizza

Sgt. Murr was our replacement for squad leader several times when Rod was otherwise occupied. He was a good man, whom I often got into trouble. Once, while transporting the CSM, I told him in detail how to properly clear his weapon, implying that he was doing it wrong. I got a commendation, and he got a lecture. All of this to a guy who I genuinely liked.

Long story short, I felt bad. So, when I went to Bagram for a class, I asked him if there was anything I could bring back for him. For some reason, he asked for a pizza. Bagram is not like a real deployment. Bagram is deployment light. It has coffee shops and other amenities not readily available in a war. One of which being pizza hut, or at least the local equivalent thereof.

So, on my last day before I head back, I pick up a pizza. Red air. Too dangerous to fly. I split the pizza with those around me and went to bed, repeating the process on the next day. Red air again. Storm front had moved into the base, didn't look like we were flying out. I caught a ride with a convoy headed in the same direction. Problem was, there was not enough room for a full pizza in the MRAP. I wrapped individual slices in foil and threw it in my pack.

One hundred and sixteen miles of the most dangerous stretch of highway imaginable. I was part of a route clearance package convoy. Their sole purpose in life was to get blown up by IEDs in specialized vehicles so others wouldn’t face as much risk. While we didn’t face any explosions this trip, we did face a few potshots from the local populace. Nothing serious enough to call an engagement, as fire was not returned.

Five hours later, we got there. Hours of occupying the same space as used underwear and socks. The pizza was less than fresh. True to my word though, I gave it to him. To my surprise, he ate it. I am not sure if I was filled with disgust or admiration. I felt somewhat accomplished though, and I remember to this day, the world's most dangerous pizza delivery. Eat your heart out Papa John.

Bicycle

It is not all doom and gloom, oh dauntless reader. There are highlights. Moments of true human connection that transcend language and culture barriers. As with other positive stories, I find that this one centers around the children. This maybe says more about me and my biases than anything else. It is easy for me to hate an adult. They know what they are doing.

With kids, it's hard for me to hate. Any Ill behavior or attitude likely stems from circumstances beyond their control. Much like my life in Afghanistan.

This happened in those short blissful days of fall when the weather was perfect. The kind of day that you could do anything with. A small breeze kept it from being too warm, carrying with it the rich scent of freshly baked bread. The sunlight bathed everything in a warming glow. The sort of idyllic day you would expect in a commercial about cigarettes or herpes medication. Yes sir, (or ma'am, or I suppose whatever the non binary honorific is for those who prefer they/them. I hope you realize that I have gone to great lengths to not exclude anyone, there is no need for thanks though because I already have your money... you got my book at the library, then get a job and buy my book, you fucking freeloading asshole) that was a beautiful day.

The only downside to this day is I was stuck on patrol. Worse yet, a walking patrol through the city. In spite of this, the weather ensured that if not a good time, at least it was not an unpleasant one. We had stopped in front of a bakery while SFC Rose spoke to one shopkeeper or another. Although I was out on the street, I could tell you exactly what was asked. The same tired questions that everybody asked. *Do you know where the*

Taliban is? Do you know where they will be? Do you have any weapons? These questions generally did not get us very far, but for some reason, we were stopped here longer than normal.

Normally, when we walked through a town, we were given a wide berth. It was almost like people did not want to attract the attention of armed invaders that didn't speak the language. The exact opposite holds true for children. Like ants at a picnic, they came. First one, then two, then swarms as they saw it was safe. Given the sheer amount of troops in such a small location, it was safe to engage a little. I handed out pieces of candy in my pockets. They introduced me to a game with a hoop and a stick, I guess the object was to keep the hoop rolling without tipping over. I traded away my green army patrol cap for a white Muslim hat. (Please forgive my ignorance in the naming, but I honestly just don't know what else to call it. It looks like a bellhop hat, but also it doesn't, so…)

All of this was done organically, with none of us speaking the language of the other. Laughter abounded as I tried to spin the hoop hula style, and applause when I finally got it right. It was the kind of wanton abandon and joy that only the really young could achieve. The penultimate event was me riding a rickety bicycle in full armor and boots. Oh, how they laughed and cheered at that. Unfortunately, this attracted the wrong sort of attention as SFC Rose came out from his meeting.

"LeClaire, off the bike, now."

That was it. I didn't get in trouble or anything. I had just had to cease my activities. This was probably the closest I ever was to winning hearts and minds. It is hard for me to hate the Afghani people because of moments like this. I picture them trapped in the same shitty situation that I was in. Torn between opposing forces, neither of which really fighting for them. Moments like this one make me wish I could take my family there and share in the openness and acceptance of the people. Sometimes a beautiful culture indeed.

Feast

Oh, vainglorious reader, you think you know what it means to feast. You picture a veritable cornucopia of food and drink. In your mind's eye, your cup runneth over and exotic dishes abound. You are wrong. You have lost sight of the true meaning of the word. From the wisdom of Elton John, "Once we were heroes, once we were kings." Well, at this time, at this place, we had managed to reclaim that, and for the first, and possibly only, period in my life, I had feasted.

It begins with the shattering your ethnocentric preconceived notions. A feast is not just an abundance of food. It is more than that, it is primal. Go back to the days of the caveman where men returned from the hunt after risking life and limb, to finally eat their fill. Flash forward to a successful raiding party where the food and spoils are shared among friends and family. Then off to the Roman Empire when, after facing down the Germanic hordes, soldiers gathered around a fire to enjoy a meal of hare or venison.

Feast comes from the Latin word festus, meaning joyous. A feast is not about the amount of food, although, ideally, you should be able to eat your fill. A feast is an occasion to celebrate, but it is also so much more. In order to have a feast, you have to overcome adversity. It is not enough to just mark a milestone of a birthday, living a year is no big accomplishment in and of itself. I have feasted after having survived for a single day or a single mission. It is the culmination of the day's events that make something noteworthy… feast worthy. It is also not something that should mark a single individual. One cannot feast by oneself. It requires camaraderie, companionship.

Usually the kind of bond that is shared amidst those who have stared death in the face and said “not today.”

It is a joining of equals, each man a king or hero in their own right, bringing stories to bear and epics to tell. Rank and status might differ from individual to individual but not at this hallowed time. During a feast, you can all share each other’s joy and delve into each pain as if it was your own. Each person adding to the collective celebration, enhancing the group and experience.

I pray, cherished reader, that, one day, you too will be able to experience a feast. Perhaps you already have, although I doubt it. On that day, be sure to mark it as the experience it is, giving it all due reverence and importance. Like all things in life, the moments are fleeting, and you will be unable to turn back the clock.

I could tell you of specific meals. I could tell you what I ate, and who I talked to. I could roll out minute by minute the best times of my life. I won’t do that. Those minutes are mine. Those glories are only to be shared with those who lived through it and fought beside me. In my infinite hypocrisy, I can only give you a generalized idea, reserving the best of times for myself, hoarding these memories like a treasure, protecting them from being marred by interlopers.

We preferred to travel by day. This wasn't always the case, just the standard procedure. As a result of this unofficial, on the longer missions that were further away from our COP, we tended to stay overnight. This had several ramifications. We would have to set guards to watch over us while we slept. We would have to pack to be entirely self-reliant for a few days. Perhaps most important, at least to this part of the story, is we would have more immersion and down time amidst the local populace and its culture.

Usually, this immersion consisted of paying the local constabulary to go out onto the town and purchase copious amounts of food. The rate of exchange between the Afghan dollar and the American dollar was about forty to one at the time. So, for about ten US dollars, we could feed about twenty people. Ten to twelve of us and eight to ten of the locals. The meals were carried on large metal plates and big metal pressure cookers with a wrapped handkerchief filled with bread, tied hobo style. Rice, with spice and lamb, beans, lentils, curry, goat, chicken, footbread, all popular dishes, served family style in heaping plates on the ground. We would sit around them, using the bread as a makeshift fork, pinching out the parcels of meat or packets of rice. No individual plates or flatware were provided. They weren't needed.

Talk and laughter filled the air as stories were recounted and exchanged. Cross cultural bridges were built as we each attempted to communicate with the others. Walls between gender, class, and even language came tumbling down under the onslaught of camaraderie and good food. To top it all off was the tea. Oh, the tea. I would gladly pay, even today, hundreds of dollars, for just one more glass of that humble tea.

Goat

I think, oh unassailable reader, that up until now, we have been working on unnamed missions. This means little to you now, perhaps, so let me illustrate the difference between named and unnamed. Despite what you may have heard or thought about how the US operates in war, at least when we deployed, we operated under a theory of self-defense. We paraded up and down the streets, in hopes that someone would attack us, and we could respond with overwhelming force. This has the benefit of A) proving they are bad guys, and B) gives us the illusion of acting with nonaggression. Unnamed missions usually fall into this category.

A named mission, at least in my experience, has a bad guy, a target, something to seek and destroy. When you hear operation so and so, you know shit's about to go down. Most of my time was spent on unnamed missions, and, as such, probably of little import to the generals who ran this war. This one however, was not. This mission was named.

What the mission was named is immaterial. I don't need you fact checking me. Additionally, I don't remember what it was named, only that it was. This was a big deal.

It all started the night before. Other squads and platoons full of people began to roll into FOB Gardez. This was atypical, to say the least. We normally had operated in single squads, with the rare occasion of two squads teaming up to accomplish different missions in the same area. This allowed us to support each other if required. For all of us to be in the same place had not happened since our first night in the country.

That night, the squad leaders were called to the brief. The mission would be on a scale that was previously unimaginable to me. Over two hundred American soldiers crammed into over forty support vehicles. Apaches provided air support. Blackhawks were on standby for medivac and detainee ops. This was to be effin awesome. For the first time in my deployment, we were going proactive, and in overwhelming force.

Machine guns and grenade launchers as far as you can see. Pure American muscle behind pure American firepower. A sight beautiful enough to make a grown man cry. Oh, and the Mk19. A forty-millimeter grenade launcher machine gun. Yes, you read that right. A machine gun with grenades for bullets. My dick can only get so erect.

The mission was to go into a town that American forces had never been able to go to before and systematically search and clear the whole thing. Like, the whole damn thing, thousands of people. Every military age male was to be run through biometrics, every house searched. Each squad had a different task.

Luckily, our squad drew clearing. Where the action was. Break into houses, bag and tag bad guys, find the weapons caches. The thrill, the rush, the pure surge of unadulterated adrenaline. There is nothing more exciting than going through a door armed for bear and ready to kill. There is nothing more terrifying than bursting through a door without knowing who or what is going to kill you on the other side.

This dichotomy of emotions, I'd say, is the most quintessential of army experiences. Love and excitement perfectly interchangeable with fear and loathing into a maelstrom of what it means to live. So, with equal parts trepidation and anticipation, we moved forward to accomplish mission.

Other squads provided an outer cordon to prevent people from entering our battlespace, completely encircling the town with vehicles and overwhelming firepower. A make-shift command center was set up, with satellite communications and real time data from drones overhead. Civilians were rounded up and put through processing stations where American soldiers collected fingerprints, names, histories, and retina scans.

Soft knock entrances were the flavor of the day. This really just meant we announced ourselves before entering and tried the door handle. This, as opposed to a hard knock, which involved breaking or blowing the door and throwing flashbangs. There are advantages and disadvantages to both. Personally, I prefer hard knock entering, as I felt a whole lot safer with the element of surprise on my side.

I digress, dear reader. I must admit my emotions run rampant on this one, and this particular memory comes in flashes. I will attempt to put some semblance of order.

It was zero dark thirty, this just meaning some time before the sun rises in the morning. We had the whole town surrounded. Helicopters whirled overhead. Mortars were set to target key intersections. My team consisted of Sgt East, Pistols, Mango, and myself.

The first two buildings we clear are empty. Single room qalats with a single lightbulb hanging from a wire and a rug trying desperately to cover an otherwise bare concrete floor. The next, had a small family huddled in the backroom. The mother shielding her children from me as if I was some foreign armed invader instead of the nice guy that I am.

It was the fourth building where things started to get interesting. It was a bigger building with several rooms. The third room in was completely bare except for a large rug. This in itself was not particularly troublesome, as we have come across the same thing several times already, but this rug wasn't laying flat. It was bulged in the middle. So, with the help of my squad, I rolled the rug back to reveal a trap door.

Time slowed. Sights got sharper when adrenaline began to course through my veins. A secret door. I vividly remember the smell of dust and spiced goat. The grit of the dirt on the handle. The taste of sweat from my brow. This was the time. Silence reigned as we prepared for entry. The door was clear of wires, no obvious signs of IEDs. There could still have been a shooter lying in wait. Order was set, position was radioed in.

I was first in line. I opened the door and cut quickly to the side so the potential first burst might miss me. Mango came next with the SAW (squad automatic weapon, in this case, an M 249), bringing considerable firepower to bear on any situation. North dove in the room, quickly cutting left to clear any threats hiding in corners. Pistols operated the same as North, only cutting right in a perfect ballet of armed protection. Systematically clearing the room of any danger.

This basement was empty save for a small window on the far wall. Mango held security over that hole, prepared to unleash hell should anything untoward appear. By virtue of my size, I was elected to go through the hole. Even with my trim, war hardened body, I was too big. After dropping body armor, I could squeeze through, but it was a tight fit.

The window/hole was about three feet thick. Through it, I could see a wall on the far side and on the right. Like it was a corner. I went in the dark. No sense in letting the enemy pinpoint my location when at my weakest, maneuvering tight corridors and dropping to the floor with no body armor. I dropped to the floor, gun scanning back and forth for any hint of terrorist lurking in the dark.

There was movement. I screamed, “Don’t you dare fucking move. I got you, motherfucker.” Something brushed up against my leg. “Goddamn Sonofabitch.” I fumbled with my rifle. The safety had gotten switched on during the transition. North threw in a chemlight. Probably in preparation for his own trip through the wall. Then I saw them. Goats. At least a hundred baby goats. I had disturbed their nap?

The noise came on. The light came on as North entered the room with his flashlight. I sat down (probably goat shit on the butt of my pants... probably). The rush was over, and now the crash. I was exhausted. Like I just ran a marathon exhausted. Completely drained and emotionally spent, I just started to laugh. Sitting in a dark room surrounded by baby goats hidden though doors and windows and under rugs, I laughed.

“You cracking up on me, Preacher man?” North asked

“Nah, be right with you, Sergeant,” I exclaimed. We searched the room. There was nothing there. No other ways in, no other ways out. To this day, I have no idea the purpose of the baby goat room. For a long time afterward, I was held to account for my actions by my “friends.”

Calls of “Watch out, Preacher there’s a goat over here,” or “ Oh my God, a goat, should we shoot it?” mocked me for months. Eventually, time marched on, and it was forgotten. Till now, when I imagine the phone calls and emails from old friends will start up again. I look forward to the inevitable goat noises and jokes I am soon to face. Thanks for that, dear reader.

40 Mph

There are three relevant pieces of information you will need to understand for this next story, the first of which being—boys are stupid. I am sure the girls are too, but as they are not featured in this part of the story, it is unimportant. Being given a gun and sent to another country no more makes you a man than your first snow cone. It is also important to note that it is boys, plural. The stupidity of a boy is synergistic with the stupidity of other boys. Meaning, the stupidest acts known to mankind are usually conceived in a group of boys.

The second piece of information you need to understand is—boys have testicles. Gender identity and all that mess aside, the boys I am talking about all have testicles. Getting hit in said testicles hurts, a lot. Like a lot, a lot. I have heard it is one of the most intensive pains a man can experience. While I have not experienced every pain humanly possible in my life, I personally can attest that it ranks up there with root canals and kidney stones.

It has been said that getting hit in the testicles ranks with and perhaps even surpasses the pain of childbirth. I cannot verify the veracity of that statement, but I can provide the logic in which it was given. A man will not ask to be hit in the testicles again throughout a normal life, provided he isn't some form of deviant. However, multiple women, many of whom are very sane, ask to have yet another baby.

The third and final piece of information you will need is that our medic, Kelly, was really into RC cars. Super into them, as a relative adult. I guess that the sport of RC cars gets more serious as you grow older. Why, he had one about the size of a loaf of bread that could go 40 miles per hour. From here, you should be able to extrapolate the gist of the story, but life is about more than just the gist, so I am going to tell it anyway.

Your humble hero and protagonist savant came in late to the scene. As such, I have no idea how this started or why. I suppose I could make up a reason and provide you an epic back story, but who has the time or the energy for that. Furthermore, oh wise reader, I am sure you remember that I would never lie to you.

I was walking back from chow with Pistols as we happened across a large group of boys from our platoon at the basketball court. In a side note, I am not exactly sure why there was a half size concrete court on base as I had never seen any basketballs, nor had the time to fuck around with them should they magically appear.

"Duuuude… You gotta come watch this," said Mango in what I thought was a little drawn out sort of way.

"What's up?" Pistols responded, ever the diplomat.

"Kelly is going to drive his RC car into Skel's nuts,"

"What? Why?"

"For forty dollars, Kelly is going to drive his RC car into Skel's nuts. It goes forty miles per hour," Mango exclaimed, as if this explained away any questions that may have arisen.

I felt, and, perhaps, still feel, like this leaves a lot to be answered. I guess forty dollars is forty dollars, and a free show is better than going back to my room. I pulled up to see Skels sitting with his back against the basketball post, legs spread wide, hands holding the pole behind his back. He shouted to the crowd, asking if anyone else wanted to give him more money. Not a very good business proposition, as he had already agreed to do it. Shockingly, there were no takers.

Kelly started his car. It sounded mean considering it was no larger than a cat. Like a lightning bolt, off it went. Rapidly, it gained speed, until—crash... Skels just went silent. You could physically watch the color drain from his face. He leaned over to the side and began puking. Cheers erupted. There was an attempt to lift Skels onto shoulders, but it was quickly abandoned as he was still dry heaving. Kelly handed him his just reward.

As quickly as it happened, it was over. People milled about, but slowly filtered out. Later that night, Skels showed me his bruise. “It barely got me in the balls,” he said proudly. “Instead it mostly hit me here in my thigh.” A deep purple and yellow bruise was all over his leg. I thought that it definitely looked like more than forty dollars-worth of pain. Oh well, you know what they say, pain is temporary, but that video is going to last forever.

Later on, after the deployment, he took his own life. Him getting hit in the nuts is one of only three videos I have of him. Damn.

Leave

Reader, I am forewarning you to skip this chapter. This chapter has nothing to do with my deployment, and you will find no war stories here. Instead, I find myself in need of a break, a brief respite against the mental and physical strain of telling my story. So, in that, I will regale you with my own tale of respite from war. The tale of my leave. My two weeks home in the middle of war.

I took my leave early. It wasn't really my choice. We had to take leave in a way that would not leave the squad critically short manned or unable to accomplish mission. I gave my rifle to the TOC where it was locked up for the duration of my leave. I kept my 9 mil up until the moment I got on the plane to get out of the country.

One of the disconcerting things about leave, is you do it alone. For months, you work in groups. If you go to the shitter, you take a buddy. Now, I was all alone, riding helicopters from base to base, trying to get to bagram. Which is another weird thing. You go to the airport, ask if they have any free spaces on a flight getting you to wherever, and they take you. No tickets, no ID, no nothing. Just hop on a plane or helicopter. It takes a few days, but I made it to bagram.

From there, it was off to Kuwait. I won't say much about this, only it was the hottest place I have ever been in my life by far, and I used to live in Phoenix. I stepped off the jet, pouring sweat. Mistakenly, I thought it was just the jet wash that was making me hot, but when I stepped out of the way of the wash, it got even hotter. Most of my time spent there, I was asleep during the day and awake at night. This actually helped in terms of jet lag I would have faced at home. One great thing to say about Kuwait, the chow was on point. Also, I don't consider

Kuwait a real deployment. So, if you or someone you know is deployed there, I just wanted to say… From the bottom of my heart, fuck you. This, of course, probably spoken more out of jealousy than anything else.

Next stop was London. I got caught in Heathrow Airport for a night when my flight was cancelled. I saw someone pull out a wallet, and a fifty-pound note immediately dropped it on the ground only to be picked up by a stranger, the original owner none the wiser. Funny what you remember. Next stop was Atlanta. Our plane was mostly military. They had fire trucks wash off the plane. I guess a symbolic gesture of cleaning away the influences or atrocities of war? Mostly I was just upset about the extra delay. It is hard to waste an extra ten minutes of my time home because someone thought it would be a great photo opportunity to wash off the plane. Must have been an officer's idea.

People stopped me on my way to my next gate, thanking me for my service. I thought this was a nice sentiment, but damned inconvenient as I was just trying to get home. Already growing weary of people thanking me for my service, I made way to the gate. I wasn't due out until the following morning, but a stroke of good luck got me onto a redeye to Phoenix. I arrived in the early morning.

My family was waiting for me past the security checkpoint. My new wife, my mother, both brothers, and one of their friends. They were all wearing matching Old Navy shirts and waving American flags. Seemed like a bit of a wasted effort. I was more interested in normalcy than some misguided attempt at patriotism. At that moment in time, I felt like I had given enough to Uncle Sam, he didn't need my R&R leave too.

It had been several years since I had seen my family, having been stationed in Germany since 2007. The first thing you remember is how much you love them, followed soon after by your second memory of how much you hate them. For lunch, we went to a restaurant named Sweet Tomatoes. Some sort of all you can eat salad buffet. I don't eat salad, and I hate buffets. The idea that everybody can stick their grubby little hands into food you will put on your plate disgusted me.

More than that, I think my family expected the boy who was sent off to war when I came home. I was far from that young man on my arrival. I was angry, bitter, and anxious. The conversation was tense and stilted. Things that they told me I cared about didn't matter to me at all. I spent a few days in town with them. I went to a Blink 182 concert with my wife. Saw Fall Out Boy and Anberlin. Went to the zoo. It was fine, but it lacked something. I think in this, I was searching for a reason to be fighting for my country.

Against familial desires, I packed up my wife and skipped town. For me, it was time to see some of this country that I was fighting for. We ended up in San Diego, California. The perfect city for me. If you have yet to experience a sunset over the pier, you have yet to experience life. San Diego was and is a city of promise for me. Weather that would be just on the verge of being too hot if not for an ocean breeze, carrying with it the scent of freshly made tortillas.

I spent lazy days on idyllic beaches, with day trips to Hollywood or Santa Monica for touristy things. At the world-famous Chinese theatre, I discovered me and Matt Damon have the same size hands, my shoes are a bit bigger though, just saying. (Although, to be fair, I would imagine his bank account is quite a bit larger than mine.) My wife and I hiked up Mt. Soledad and fed sea lions at SeaWorld. On the sea lions, if you ever want to feed them, make sure the throw is directly at them, baseball style. Believe me, they can catch it. If you throw too high, seagulls will snatch them out of the air.

This was truly one of the best times of my life, but as quickly as it came, it left. Before I could blink, the time was over, and I had to head back to Afghanistan. We drove back to

Phoenix. I hugged my mother and brothers goodbye. I gave my wife a kiss and headed down through that long security tunnel at the airport. My family was all crying. I didn't look back for fear that they would see me cry too.

I joke with my son sometimes that I had my tear ducts surgically removed in Afghanistan. I didn't need them, and they were just taking up space. Obviously, this is a farce, the surgeons in Bagram would not perform such an unsafe and elective surgery. Perhaps this day, more than any other, was my affirmation of the truism men don't cry. Healthy or not, nothing is served by falling victim to your grief. You do not best serve your family by breaking down in front of them. As a man, you owe your family more than that. Grief is a luxury afforded to women and children.

Apple

Shortly after my leave, or perhaps shortly before, my squad was doing an overnight at the local police station. I say local, and I am sure it was local to someone, but it sure as shit wasn't us. Local police is how we verbally differentiated between border police and military police. So please don't read local as a locational tag, rather a mark of who they were. A badge of ineptitude if you will. There I go, off on another tangent. Long story, short. We were on an overnight trip, four hours out of base, dealing with the local police.

There was not a whole lot for most of us to do on these trips. We brought twelve soldiers and one interpreter, which means ninety percent of the time, eleven of us had nothing to do. Sure, we would pull security or spend the odd bit of time trading with the ANP, Afghan National Police. Boys being boys, we would on occasion get to daring each other to do stunts of increasing stupidity.

It all started with a deck of cards. Myself, Pistols, Chile, and Crackers were playing a rousing game of Spades whilst sitting by a small campfire. Our makeshift MRE box table was just big enough for the four of us to sit around and make bids or take books. These things, of course, being things that you do in the game of Spades. The sun had just risen, and the heat for the day had not yet set in. Clouds drifted idly overhead. The smell of cooking food and the sounds of waking people wandered in as the world slowly woke up around us.

In spite of this, I was frustrated. Pistols had underbid again, causing us to lose points. The thing you should know about Pistols is he was a great dude. He would give you the shirt of his back and walk with you through hell, but he was a terrible card player. I can forgive a lot of things, but I was unsure if I could forgive this mess he was getting me in. Lord help us if we lose to Crackers and Chile. I would never hear the end of it.

Luckily, I was saved from this humiliating defeat. Crackers' watch beeped angrily at him. "Gotta jet, my dudes, my shift," Crackers announced as he stood up. "We will continue this ass whuppin' tonight." He gestured toward the cards.

"In your dreams. Me an' Pistols have you right where we want you," I said, knowing full well I intended to lose the score sheet as soon as possible so we could start again fresh. Chile, perhaps wise to my intentions, grabbed the sheet from the box.

"I'll just hold this then, till we play tonight. So we can pick up right where we left off," Chile replied dryly. A hint of smugness had crept into his voice. Of the Spade duos, Chile and Crackers were the worst. A title I did not wish to claim. Crackers laughed as he walked away.

"So…" Pistols let his voice trail off, making it more of a question than a statement. "What now?" This was a harder question than it seemed. We had very little in means of ways to entertain ourselves. There were not a lot of card games designed for three people. I was also remarkably unprepared for this endeavor. In future missions, I would always make sure I brought my Game Boy or kindle.

"Well, shit, man. If you need your hand held so badly, why don't you go hold his?" Chile asked as he pointed to a member of the ANP, thus starting a new game. Some clarification on this point. Typically, the ANP smelled poorly, as they practiced what Americans would call poor hygiene. Hand holding was especially extra, because it would put you in close proximity. Also, you do not know the language. A good portion of them might misconstrue it as you were hitting on them. They might call you a chai boy, which is what they called male sex slaves. All around, a wonderful bet and a terrible idea.

Pistols, however, had no shame and no fear. He marched straight up to the Afghani and took his hand. He then led him back to us, more than half pulling him along. The man looked confused as he let himself be dragged by this diminutive American soldier. Pistols motioned for him to sit on the cot with us, then offered him an MRE. The man, probably not understanding what was going on, took it and smiled. Chile and me chuckled a bit at the sight, as the Afghani took his food, stood up, and left, smiling and waving the whole time, all the while mumbling in a language we didn't understand.

"Done," Pistols said. He looked around for a dare that he could pass on and return the favor. "Hey, Preacher, why don't you go get me an apple?" This dare was even more loaded then the last. A woman was carrying a bushel of apples over to her home. As a whole, Afghanistan is rather protective of their women, and who knows what kind of offense I would cause trying to get an apple.

I had a bit of a cheat though. I waved over one of the many, many kids that always seemed to hang around. Four came. "Pen? Candy?" I asked. The children nodded and murmured in excitement. "I give you pen, candy, you give me apple," I said slowly and loudly as if that would somehow break the language barrier. I pointed to the lady and pantomimed eating an apple. "Trade. Pen. Candy. Apple," I said, trying to will the exchange through my voice and motions.

Even with my fumbling and feeble attempts at communication, one of them understood me and raced off to accomplish the task. I proudly traded this small child a brand new Bic and a few jolly ranchers I kept solely for these purposes.

"Here ya go, Pistols. An apple." Chile laughed, frankly reminding me that he was still there. "Why don't you go feed this apple to that cow over there, Chile?" I handed him the apple. "With your mouth."

"What?" Chile asked.

"No hands, dude. Bite the apple. Let the cow eat it out of your mouth," I replied.

Chile took the apple. He said, "Easy," as he sauntered over toward the cow. The cow just eyed him with those cow eyes devoid of life or interest. Chile put the apple in his mouth and reached out toward the cow. The cow saw the apple for the first time and reached out its tongue for a taste.

Right as the two met, Rod yells out, "What the fuck is going on here?"

Chile dropped the apple in surprise. "Nothing, Sergeant. Just feeding a cow."

Rod looked at Chile strangely, then, deciding it wasn't worth the conversation, barked out his orders. "Pack your shit. We are headed down to the city to set up a checkpoint. That goes for you guys too."

With that, the moment was over. I picked up my gun and got back to work. I knew the people beside me were doing the same. My old drill sergeant used to say, never stand when you can sit. Never sit when you can lay down. Never lay down when you can sleep. I took this to mean do what you can, while you can do it. We were able to carve out a moment of levity in an otherwise shitty time. This was... this is still, just as important as anything else you might read here.

Bootleg

Oh, contemptuous reader, how we revel in the illicit and illegal. The pure unadulterated thrill of doing something wrong and getting away with it. The adrenaline that goes along with the immoral. Why does no one tell you that being bad feels oh so good. Today, I want to tell you of the simplest of slights, an everyday evil, in which I am sad to say that I enjoyed often and with great fervor. Copyright infringement.

Intellectual property seemingly does not exist in Afghanistan. Short of the American run Bx/PX on Bagram air base, I do not recall seeing a single movie, CD, or video game that was not some form of bootleg. This offers both an upside, and a down. Most goods cost between one and five dollars a disc. Some of them were perfect quality, and you couldn't tell it from a regular store bought one.

Some movies in particular were in somewhat rougher condition. Some were handheld video cameras in theatres. Some were leaked copies in various stages of the editing process. For instance, I watched X Men, Wolverine (a heavily CGI featured action movie) without any form of CGI or green screen. While it did make for an interesting behind the scenes look at how movies are made, the story itself is somehow lessened without backdrop in most scenes and tons of MoCap guys running around. Some I purchased were blank or had viruses. Overall, the thrill of a steal had me and countless others going back.

There existed several places or means to secure such illicit products. On COP Herrera, we had to rely on the Terps or ANP to go out and bring us back the goods. This was obviously not the ideal situation, as who knows what they want to watch without spending time browsing all the available titles. Additionally, prices were extremely negotiable. DVDs that started off at ten dollars might be purchased ten for a dollar. With someone else handling the exchange, you lost the ability to make those deals.

The other option was more rare. Walking foot patrol through the market. This happened on occasion, but in order for you to make a deal, you would have to be stationary in a threat rich environment. The amount of times we had stopped on a foot patrol in a place where I could make a purchase and a stop long enough to make said purchase, I can count those on one hand.

In the larger bases, however, the powers that be bring in locals and vet their goods for a miniature market on base. This was the tits. Creme da la creme. Plenty of things at great prices in the relative safety of a military base. This, of course, had its own drawbacks and challenges, but those were faced primarily on the bigger picture guys, not the individual consumer like me.

As it turned out, one of our trusted interpreters was running some sort of protection racket with the people who ran the stalls—my mob knowledge, purely derived from a viewing of the Godfather a decade ago, forgive me if I get any of the terminology wrong. So, this dude, we will call him Terpy, had it rigged so those who paid him got to stay and work on the FOB. Those who didn't pay had a tendency to get wrapped up in suspected terrorism plots and were forced off in short order.

This being my only real encounter with some sort of organized crime, I found it remarkably convenient. If you thought you were getting an unfair deal, or the shit you bought didn't work, you just went to Terpy, and he took care of it. One stop shop for all your needs, really. Broken systems really only seem broken when you're on the wrong side of things.

Prep

I know, dear reader, that I tend to gloss over things that I find uninteresting or routine. Most likely, you are not a trained soldier, and, as such, unaware of the prep work that goes into a mission. In order to form a more perfect union of our two minds, I would like to fill in some of the blanks now.

Most missions were planned in advance, and we would know about it the night before. As a gunner, my job entailed preparing the back of the truck. I would ensure that I had the proper combat load of ammunition to my crew served weapon. Then I would ensure that I had at least one box of MREs, most of the time we brought two, as some of them are inedible. I would pack cases of water, at least two, usually four. Then I would fill up two five-gallon drums with drinking water, mostly for emergencies, but we had also used them for makeshift showers on longer ops. I would swing through the TOC and make sure I had any propaganda pamphlets I would be passing out for PSYOPs.

Inside the truck, I would make sure I had my pintle mount for a regular truck and, most importantly, the pintle pin. The pin is theoretically supposed to be chained to the mount, but hardly ever was. On CROWS vehicles, I would check my wires and make sure everything was running correctly, powering it up and giving it a dry test run.

After the truck was prepped, I would see to my personal gear. A quick run of cleaning on my personal weapons and the truck weapon I would be taking the following day. I would go through my ammunition and make sure that it was filled. Next, I would double check my first aid kit. Finally, I would check my assault bag for the miscellaneous things that I might need. This included charged Game Boy, book, Clif Bars, and the all-important crystal light single serve lemonades.

The driver ran the truck and made sure the radios and FBCB2 was in working order. The night before, he (or she, but in my case, it was exclusively a dude, and so I will refer to drivers as he) would fill the gas tank, as well as separate gas cans. They made sure the truck was in good working order. Frankly, I have no idea what this entails, as I was not then, nor have I ever been, a driver.

In the morning, if I had time, I would grab chow, including a to go plate for my squad leader who was undoubtedly in a pre-mission brief. I would mount the truck weapon and double check everything was tied down. I would grab Ssg Rod's gear and load it up for him, not because I had to, I just had the time, and he didn't. It was one of the many ways that teamwork makes the dream work.

The driver would fill the radios (some sort of techno wizardry that allowed us to talk to each other without the enemy being able to intercept) and do a com check. He would also do a quick double check making sure everything was in working order. Then we would meet up in front of the truck and wait on our mission briefing. This was where we learned specifically what we were doing for the duration of the mission. Most days included some sort of mission, so this was pretty routine for us.

Gym

On the gym in COP Herrera was a sign that said, “the small arms repair shop.” I loved that. I am not a gym rat. I would venture to say that before I joined the military, I had never been in a gym, and after, I haven’t returned. It was a matter of free time. I had a massive amount of it, and it irked me to no end. I found that a great way to get to sleep at night, or at least a way to quiet a troubled mind, was to spend time at the gym.

There is a peace that you can find by taking some useless hunk of heavy metal and lifting it up. Then setting it down. Over and over. The strain of the work on the machine of your body often overrides any machinations the mind might have.

When I deployed, I weighed in at 190 lbs. I returned at 160. None of my clothes fit. I was far from the only one this had happened to. Small guys came back big, big guys came back small. Jacked guys came back absolutely shredded. If you, my unsatisfied reader, are unhappy with your current body physique, I highly recommend joining the Army and deploying to Afghanistan.

For the first time, I learned gym etiquette. There are a myriad of rules and customs that must be followed or risk punishment. Weights should be racked on completion. Equipment should be wiped down when done with it. Talking is limited to body related questions and answers and kept to a minimum. If you don't know how something works, ask, but don't expect someone to interrupt their routine to babysit you. If they so deign to help you, thank them, and move on. It is okay to ask for a spot or work in with someone. This is where you take turns on a machine. Most people take a short rest between sets. Because of this resting period, it is imperative that you ask if someone is done with a machine before you jump on. Finally, don't slam the weights to the floor when you're done. At one point or another, I seem to have fucked up all of these things, only to be immediately censured with dirty looks and an occasional "What the fuck, man?"

It is important to bring music and headphones. I personally preferred hard rock for weights and rap for cardio but do whatever works for you. This is very important, as whatever music playing over the loudspeaker will be impossible to work out to. I swear I heard Dolly Parton before. I split pretty evenly between weights and cardio, alternating every other day and taking Sundays off. Hopefully, these insights will save you from some of the pitfalls I have had in the gym.

Being downrange had its own special perks and challenges in regard to a gym. Sometimes, we would bench three fifty-cal barrels taped together. We would carry ammos cans instead of kettlebells. Our running route was carefully mapped out and taped off to avoid the active landmines that were still on the COP.

One particular day stands out in memory. I had just finished a vexing mission, which, through no fault of me or mine, had resulted in a kid's death. It turned out that the local aggressors seemed a lot less interested in protecting civilian life than we were. This in and of itself was nothing special. A sad but common truth to conflict. For some reason though, I couldn't shake his face. The dull eyes, the all too still chest. He looked like a discarded toy as opposed to a kid gunned down running for cover.

I was working on my bench press. "*Let the bodies hit the floor*" lift the bar "*Let the bodies hit the floor,*" lower the bar. "*One, nothing's wrong with me,*" up. "*Two, nothing's wrong with me,*" down. "*Three, nothing's wrong with me,*" up. "*Four, nothing's wrong with me.*" So, it went, the song on repeat. For what might have been thirty minutes, but could also have been an eternity, till I could physically lift the bar no more. My chest and arms on fire, I had been exercised and exorcised. The needs of my physical body effectively blocking emotions I was incapable of dealing with.

I am no expert in therapy or stress disorders. Hell, I am barely able to cope with these conditions most days. I can say that of all of the shit I have seen or done, this is one of the incidents that bother me the least. Perhaps there is something to be said about depression and anxiety being lessened through exercise and activity. I am sure people much smarter than you or I, dear reader, will figure it out.

Rip it

The war may have been persecuted and practiced by troops, but it was fueled by Rip it. Rip it is an off-brand energy drink provided en-mass to troops. It is like you take a red bull and remove all of the flavor. A straight kick in the gut. It was also essential. Many a truck included a case of rip it as a standard load item. It's hard to place a price on the ability to stay awake and alert in combat situations.

It was dark. More than just an absence of light, but an oppressive dark. As if it hunted down any source light and snuffed it out. It was a cold dark. A winter's night with a winter's bite. The cold sapped at strength and energy, removing the will to accomplish mission and replacing it with a desire for a warm fire and home. I had been up for over forty-eight hours. Not that I wasn't afforded the opportunity to sleep. Them, they, terrorists, opposition, bad guys, whoever the fuck seemed to be on a single-minded mission to keep me awake. A series of running TICs (troops in combat, a minor engagement) followed by mortars.

My body had seemingly lost the ability to produce or react to adrenaline. Now it was the crash. Complete and utter exhaustion set in. My body was going down, and it was going down hard. The only problem is that we were away from base, and I had at least twenty-four hours before I could sleep. Then the hero of our story entered. Rip it. Liquid lightning canned for convenience.

I started to nod off and slammed a can. I took a long blink, slammed a can. By the time we were rolling out the next day, I had a small pyramid of cans, some five or six tall. Pyramid, three dimensional. I was cold and sweaty. My breathing was rapid and shallow. I stayed up, but at a terrible cost. The medic said my heart was in dysrhythmia, it was beating irregularly. Upon return to base, I was given an IV and a sedative. I had to stay at the medics for the next two days for observation. I suffered from extreme physical and psychological exhaustion. Muscles that I wasn't even aware I had screamed at me for keeping them awake.

After that day, I had a hard time drinking energy drinks. It’s as if my body has a physical rejection mechanism. Rip it still remained popular with quite a few troops. Most that I know could tell you stories similar to mine. Better living through modern chemistry, I guess. To be fair, it worked as advertised. I took it to stay awake, and stay awake I did.

Tattoo

Pistols went on leave around the same time I did. Unlike me, he had decided to get a tattoo to commemorate the occasion. As a fellow gunner, he had determined that a fifty-caliber bullet would be the perfect deployment tattoo. He got it down his forearm. Pistols being Pistols had to also attach a joke to his tattoo. Inscribed on this bullet are the words "Your Name."

When I met up with him in Bagram, literally the first words out of his mouth were, "Hey, Rodney, I went home and got a bullet with your name tattooed on it."

“Nah, man,” I said, not understanding where the joke was, but knowing it was there.

“Really, I went home and got a tattoo of a bullet with your name on it, bet.”

“Bullshit.”

“Twenty bucks.”

“Done.” He rolls up his sleeve and reveals his tattoo. Unfortunately, his tattoo artist had no idea the proportions or shape of an actual fifty cal round, and he ended up with what looked like a bullet of another type.

“Dude, you got a dildo on your arm.” For added effect, we compared the illustration to an actual round. Not even remotely close. It is definitely shaped like a vibrator. It is a running joke to tell people that Pistols has a dildo with your name on it.

Smoke

If you want to get ahead in the Army, take up smoking. Smoking is a time-honored tradition for the military. It gets you more time off work, as you routinely get smoke breaks where you spend ten to fifteen minutes sucking down cancer. It gets you facetime with people who are above you in rank and station, and lets you talk to them outside the rigid rules and regulations of everyday military life. Having cigarettes on your person to loan out provides such a benefit that I would recommend carrying a pack even if you don't smoke.

In most places I was deployed, the smoking shack was also the water pit. This was beneficial for me, as it gave me a reason to hang around even though I don't smoke. It gave me access to the kind of hip pocket mentorship that wouldn't be available otherwise. It was here that I learned what it was to be a leader, to give direction and be resolute, but at the same time have an off channel means of communication where you can listen to your subordinate's goals or concerns.

The smoking area was the routine hangout for everyone. There was hardly any time day or night, that you couldn't find some hanging out and lighting up. Cigarettes constituted a currency in their own right. I have seen ECP or KP duty changed for a carton or a few packs.

It was here in the smoke pit that I learned what it was to lead. Ssgt Baguette, would talk to us in between drags of his favored brand, Camel Silvers. Waves of knowledge washed over us as the smoke settled. "To lead is to suffer," he would spout, to anyone who was listening. "Youse all don't think I would rather be a Specialist, goofin' off with my dick in my hand? Whatcha don't understand is I'm there. I'm the guy working behind the scenes so youse don't have to. If you wanna be a leader, old boy, you gots to step up to the plate and shield those working under you. It is not about you doing less work. It's about your people being able to succeed. My soldiers need to go to boards. My soldiers need to go to schools. My soldiers will be educated. My soldiers better do better than me or I will PT them to fuckin' death."

It was exactly these words that resonated with me. To him, his soldiers were more than work subordinates or colleagues, they were his kids. His family. He showed me everything the Army could and should be. I loved him for it. These conversations, these nuggets of wisdom, only made possible through the passing of cigarettes. As if the smoke let us act and speak without the pomp and circumstance that is rank.

Combatives

Take a ton of testosterone driven young men, drop them in a warzone thousands of miles from home, and expect them to perpetrate violence on your behalf, and you can't expect everything to go smoothly all the time. Surprisingly, most of the time, it went well. Every now and then, however, we would come to moments of unavoidable friction. The dude you eat with, sleep with, and face the enemy with finally pushed you too far. During these times, we liked to solve the problem in the best way possible, by means of copious amounts of physical violence.

There is something freeing in the act of fighting. You defend your beliefs through the strength of your arm or quickness of your jab, knowing that your opponent is doing the same. Without fail, one hundred percent of the time I attempted to solve a problem with my fists, we both ended up better off for it. Me and my opponent stood and shook hands. This isn't to say I won every fight. I would say I got my ass whupped in about half of them.

There exists a set of unwritten rules and regulations for a fight downrange. They always went under the guise of combatives training. They were always mano e mano. The fight ended at pass out or tap out. Then you shake hands and walk away. The fights were always witnessed. Soldiers helping soldiers from stopping things from going too far.

Since I very carefully set up the rules of combatives training, I will now give you examples of shit that was not that. It was just me attacking, sometimes right, sometimes wrong. If you don't like my transition here, too bad. It's my story, and I already got your money soo...

Everyone has a line. A phrase or action that can set them off. For me, the line is my glasses. My glasses are mine. They are a necessity for my survival. I am legally blind. People who take my glasses or hit them from my face are liable to reap the whirlwind of my fury.

This time, it was Cliff at the smoking pit. Cliff had probably fifty pounds and six inches on me. We pretty routinely went to combatives training, with him more oft than not emerging the victor. The last time though, I had caught him in a sweet triangle choke, and he was forced to tap out. This was the topic of conversation at the pit.

He said something about me to the crowd. I said something about him to the crowd. Nothing outright, but it was obvious we were trading barbs. Then a step too far.

"Your bitch of a wife teach you that move," said Cliff in a mocking tone.

"Least I have a bitch. Bitch."

Then an openhanded slap of a sucker punch came flying in from somewhere in the back. My glasses went flying. The sharp sting on my face did nothing to soothe my seething anger. I could not see.

Luckily, Cliff was about the biggest sonofabitch out there, so when I aimed for the big one, I struck true. A glancing haymaker sent him stumbling backward on the gravel. I was on him like a hound on a bone. Haymaker after haymaker, kept him on the back step. He had stayed upright for three or four hits, then those big stupid ass feet of his got tripped up. I jumped on him, aiding his fall with my not inconsiderable weight.

I couldn't see more than two feet in front of me without my glasses, but it didn't matter anyway, as all I saw was red. At this point, it dawned on me that both me and him were carrying a loaded pistol. I couldn't say if he was reaching for his weapon or if I went to reach for mine. True friends to us both, tackled me then dragged us apart before we could unholster 9 mils.

We stood up, dusted ourselves off, and were forced to make the most tense handshake I had ever experienced. That quick sudden burst of anger was honed in Afghanistan. It has kept me alive. Now, I spend two hours a week trying to get rid of it.

PHQ

Toward the end of my deployment, some tasks and missions ventured toward the menial. The powers that be determined that we were to have a twenty-four-hour presence at the provincial police headquarters in downtown Gardez. This in and of itself is no big deal, or perhaps it was a very big deal, who am I to say. All I can say for certain, is this squad of people lived outside American wire and inside Afgan wire.

One of my favorite leaders in the world was charged to lead this ragtag group. Sgt. Coffee was everything you could and should expect out of a sergeant. To this day, I hold him in the highest regard, and my own leadership style has evolved around his teachings. He always led from the front, working alongside his men (and women) regardless of the detail. He took time to not only understand his soldiers as individuals, but to help mold them into a team. He protected his soldiers from the spray of bullshit that fell down the chain of command whenever possible, often shouldering the burden himself.

I fucking hated having to go and see him, for some asshole behind a desk thought it was a good idea to send Sgt Coffee and his men out to live at an Afghan headquarters ten minutes outside of FOB Gardez. This meant that my happy ass had to drive down and bring them hot chow. Why they couldn't drive back was a question I had often asked at volume to my leadership. The preparations and eventual take downs of these trips accounted for a good portion of what should have otherwise been free time.

Occasionally, we would eat with them. More often than not, we would pull security for them so they could eat in peace. This, in and of itself, was no big deal. Thirty minutes of work to help out a brother or sister. This minuscule break for them meant two hours in mission time for everyone on chow duty.

There isn't any deeper meaning or story here. I just wanted you to know that chow runs were bullshit, and fuck everybody who lived and worked at PHQ.

Betrayal

Winter of '09 was a violent one for me. A few troops in combat, a few more mortars, and of course the ever-present threat and explosions of IEDs. Despite this, or perhaps in spite of, my spirits remained relatively high. I had gotten a handle on war. I knew the ins and outs of violence and was comfortable with my situation. This, of course, rested on the fact that I was able to compartmentalize extremely well.

Submarines wished they had my ability to separate and segment themselves from themselves as well as I had. I was king at keeping my life separated, or so I thought. It was during this time that I had faced the ultimate betrayal from the most unlikely of sources. Fuck, that is a stupid phrase. Obviously, you can shield yourself from betrayal if you know it is coming. I think the definition of betrayal implies it must come from a loyal source. If not, it should.

The reason this betrayal worked so well is that it was from someone I never thought would betray me, doing an action in which he most likely never considered a betrayal. This particular piece of canine excrement wasn't even stationed with me, and, in fact, had very little to do with my life. It is my understanding that soldier shithead had injured himself and was sent home early for rest and recovery. How, one may ask? Or, more likely, how is this relevant information? Well, ignorant reader of mine, let me enlighten you.

PFC Caca was having a snowball fight in the middle of a warzone. He then proceeded to slip on ice and tear his MCL or his ACL.... Some sort of L was torn. He was able to have a snowball fight because he was stationed on Bumfuck Nowhere and had never seen any action. This, of course, is not a very compelling story.

Upon his arrival home, he proceeded to tell the family and friends, MY FAMILY AND FRIENDS, that he was in the shit. A hero worthy of respect. The problem with these wild and delusional fantasies of his is that they vaguely represented mine and my squad's life, as we were actually in the shit.

Like the famed walls of Jericho, my carefully constructed compartmentalization came crashing down. The lies I had told my family about how it was okay, the times I had shielded them from some terrible truth, all called into question. I was okay because my family knew that I was okay. Now that my family knew, or more likely suspected, I was not okay, what was I now?

After many talks, I would have rather not had, an uneasy compromise was reached. A compromise that seemed all too fitting given the policies set forth by the US Army. They wouldn't ask, and I wouldn't tell. Ultimately, this stopgap served no one. This knowledge only came, however, after years of self-medication and, worse yet, VA prescribed medication.

Medic

There are a few things in this world which are to be prized above all others: the love of a good woman, the Incredible Hulk issue 181 (the first appearance of wolverine, well… technically the second, since he was in the last panel of issue 180), and a friend who can keep a secret.

It was hot. Too god damn hot. (You will find this to be a running theme in this book, mainly, because in my experience with the country, I had only found two temperatures. Too hot, or too cold) Sweat poured down my brow, it stung at my eyes and blurred my vision. I lay on my bed sans clothes, except for boxers and a tan shirt. Chile called out to me.

"Yo, you got that DVD I lent you?"

"Nah man, that ain't me," I replied, ever the conversationalist.

"The fuck you mean, that ain't you?" Chile responded, his voice starting to betray the fact that he was more than a little agitated. "Who the fuck is it then?"

"Mmmm, gave it to Pistols, I think?" more a question than a statement. This loaning and passing around of DVDs was not uncommon for us at the time. And with the aforementioned cost of pirated entertainment, was not a big deal. Until it was, I guess.

"I don't give a fuck, who you gave it to, I gave it to you. You will give it back to me," Chile said, as he began to pound on my closed door.

"Calm your tits." I made my way over to the door so I could talk to him face to face as opposed to through the wooden slab that made up my door. Perhaps here, I misunderstood how angry he was. Perhaps it was the heat. Perhaps he had finally had a mental break. Regardless of the reason. The second I opened the door I was speared by a flying tackle.

I went down. Hard. A loose nail jabbed into my back as I lay on the ground, stunned. While I was still not fully comprehending what was going on, Chile disentangled himself and walked away. I got to my feet and caught up to him at his room. “You think you can just walk away from me?” I yelled. A lifetime of wrasslin’ shows had prepared me for this moment. In a move that would have done Diamond Dallas Page proud. I grabbed at Chile and DDT’ed him right onto an ammo can.

“That’s what I thought.” I called out to his still form. His still form. Chile wasn’t moving. Fuck. Pistols came out of his room.

“What the fuck you do, man? The fuck you do?” Pistols said, looking at me in horror. By this point, thirty seconds had elapsed, he was still not moving. Blood trickled from a small wound on his head.

"Stay with him, bro," I yelled over my shoulder as I tore out of the hooch. "I'mma get the medic." Fortunately for me, the medic Ash was just two hooches down. Unfortunately, he also shared his domicile with my immediate supervisor and several others who would see me worse for wear if they knew the current situation. I slowed to a walk as I entered his door.

"Ash? You in here?" I called out, praying that he wasn't on ECP or any other myriad of missions.

"What is it?"

"Yo, if we could steal you for half a second…" My voice trailed off as my brain stumbled, trying to catch up to my mouth. "We're practicing IV lines for the soldier board and could use a medic to make sure we doing this right."

Ash groaned, "I guess."

"Hold on, Ash, I'll head over with you," North said through the wall. My team leader North. Fuck. "If my soldiers are practicing for the boards, I should be there too."

"Shit, man. I forgot." I said to the wall. "Sfc Rose was looking for you. I ran into him at the DFAC ten minutes ago." This of course being a lie. The DFAC was on the other side of the FOB, and a decent size to boot. This should buy me twenty minutes at least.

"What he want?" the wall asked.

"Dunno. He told me and Pistols to do some board practice and asked me to send him you." North just groaned.

"Allright, but we gonna hit them books tonight. Let's do weapons after chow."

"Sounds good, boss!" I called back. I turned my attention back toward Ash "Yo, can you bring your kit, in case we need anything else?" Ash sighed as he shouldered his medic bag. Together we walked, perhaps too slowly, toward my door. Maybe four minutes had passed at this point.

“You need me to look at that back?” Ash said as I opened the door. He pointed at my shirt where blood was slowly starting to seep through.

“I... uh, maybe you should come inside first.”

Chile lay where we left him. Ash looked to me questioningly but went right to work. He removed a pack of ammonium carbonate, also known as smelling salts, from his bag and after opening it, wafted it under Chile’s nose. Within seconds, Chile roused from his slumber.

“The hell happened here, guys?” Ash said, looking from Chile to Pistols to me. None of us met his gaze.

“Tell you what, Ash, I got a pack of top ramen in a care package that says nothing happened here,” I said. Chile and Pistols nodded.

“Better make it three,” Ash replied, voicing his assent.

“Done and done.”

Justice

We aspire for justice. Often times, we find out that it is just us. This can be taken in a number of ways. I assure you, reader, I intend every one of them. Sometimes, justice fails. Sometimes we fail justice. We act in a way that we feel is just or right, without map or guide. Sometimes all others act in a way that is unjust, and we remain the only bulwark against the night.

It was deep winter when it happened. Under the cover of predawn darkness, ODA (read Spec Ops) infiltrated a small town. Before the sun crested the mountains, bodies lay cooling in the snow. The splashes of red in sharp contrast to a sea of white. If not for the smell of gunpowder and the lamentation of the women, it was an otherwise peaceful scene. Our platoon was on outer security and detainee Ops. ODA was a relatively small team, and having the support of a larger contingent of troops made their mission run smoother.

I was a CROW gunner in this particular mission, I was also tasked with monitoring ODA radio channels in case they called for help or needed us to reposition. I was struck by their pure professionalism as I heard the bodies start dropping. Perhaps more impressive was the amount of prisoners that they managed to take. In a world where martyrdom is a way of life, this, more than anything speaks to how good of a force they are. I would then relay this information to the LT who would dispatch a squad to sandbag the prisoner and tag him with appropriate information, who he said he was, where he was found, etc. The prisoners were then moved to a holding area on the edge of town. It is important to note that at least at the time, the US had a policy of detaining everyone and sorting them out shortly afterward. Some detainees (read prisoners) would only remain so till we had collected the appropriate information at mission end.

The entire mission was complete by sun up. I was to be part of the relief for the guards in the prisoner holding area, letting them get a chance to warm up in the truck and perhaps grab some chow. Additionally, I was one of the few soldiers trained in collecting biometric data, including fingerprints and iris scans. This would allow us to transfer the prisoners to the detention facility with a more complete set of identification.

The prisoners were being held outside the tent set up for detention. As I approached, I saw what I can only describe as pure evil. Forced to stand barefoot in the snow there wasn't a single one not suffering from some stage of hypothermia. Tan sandbags obscured vision as I saw "soldiers" dump snow on their bodies. Petty evils bestowed for no other reason but for the fact that they could. (I won't name the individual. It is my firm belief that this was on the verge of war crimes.)

"What the fuck are you doing?" I said.

In the most casual way possible, I got the reply "Just having a bit o' fun," as if there was nothing wrong with the situation at hand. The individual in question saw this activity as no different than throwing a football. I saw how the Taliban was able to gain power through the misdeeds of evil men.

I reported the situation to the LT. The "soldier" in question was reassigned, and a letter of misconduct was placed in his file. I brought the prisoners into the heated tent. After collecting biometrics, only three of the dozen or so were kept to be transferred to a detainee camp. Lady justice was blind that day.

Much later, a seemingly thirteen year-old-girl gets killed in the crossfire in a small running engagement. By the time we get back to the scene, lividity had set in. Blood pooled to the parts of her body that were closer to the ground. She was in a state of undress. I'm not sure what was said here. Looking back, I still see red. Same individual as before, comments on her tits. A dead child. Parents still mourning in the next room. The body cooling not cold.

East dragged me out of the room. I should have shot him. I guess my mission was only to eliminate evil not wearing an American flag on their shoulder. To add insult to injury, Dookie, previously mentioned, managed to get her truck stuck at the cemetery where they were trying to bury the child. We had Decepticon logos spray painted on our trucks. This incident led to a reward being offered by the Taliban on our lives. We had to remove the logos.

Justice was not always served overseas. I tried my best to operate under a certain set of principles and morality, keeping in line with the values imparted on me through my upbringing and religion. In the end, only God can judge me. Sometimes I worry that I didn't do enough. It's easy to determine right or wrong from the comforts of your own home. Fuck you, reader. Fuck you.

Packages

Over the course of my deployment, I had received several packages. I got a letter from a second grader asking me to kill all the bad guys and come home. I got a box from a church in Texas filled with mints. Literally—just mints. A large flat rate box. My wife sent me a back massager, which was sorely needed and greatly appreciated. My father sent me a box filled with chocolate and elk jerky. The chocolate was dripping from the box in a sugary mess, don't send chocolate to a desert in the middle of summer. My mother sent me a bible. One church smuggled alcohol and sent shaving supplies.

I would order crystal light single serve lemonade packages from amazon by the hundred. They were available in the chow hall, but not all flavors, or all the time. Truthfully, that was about it. I probably had gotten about ten packages my whole time on deployment. I tried sharing my spoils amidst the troops, as not everyone got letters or packages from home. Also, some days, I wouldn't get anything, and it was nice to share in someone else's spoils.

There was only one thing that I asked for that I didn't get. There is a candy we used to make around the holidays called overseas candy. The story goes, it was called this because it was able to be sent to soldiers deployed overseas during World War Two. Supposedly, it was something made for my grandfather on my mother's side during his deployment in Europe. I guess I was just hoping for a connection to a man that I never got the chance to meet.

Aid

By now, you are my compatriot. A fellow soldier in arms. You have faced many of my trials and stood beside me as I was being brought low. I don't know how to classify or forewarn you of this next story. I can merely lay it out and let you be the judge. Early in the story, I mentioned the running over of a face. If you cannot remember that far back, oh befuddled reader, then I envy you. For it has been ten long years, and I still remember the faces.

Uggh, there I go again.

This chapter is entitled aid. So, it is only just that I should cover this subject with at least some passing attempt at clarity. It is so hard to stick to a single subject when my memories start to blend and combine. A whirlwind of emotion takes over as I remember elation alongside despair. One sentence bleeds into the next, as if by letting myself be taken by a single thought, I have breached the dam, unleashing an endless torrent of good and bad. Lord help me in these coming days. As you have shown me your willpower by reading, I too can show my willpower by writing.

A large part of our mission over there was to win hearts and minds. This slogan was quickly and subtly changed by soldiers into we aim for hearts and minds. The latter being a call out to our superior marksmanship with our weapons as opposed to building meaningful relationships with the locals. Some parts of this campaign to indoctrinate the populace into a pro-American mentality was to provide humanitarian aid. Most of the time, I gave to the children. Gatorade, pens, and candy were all in high demand and can get you quick feel good reactions.

There were assholes who would subvert attempted contact or connection. I am sad to report that this occurred on both sides of the conflict. American soldiers would throw

Gatorade bottles filled with piss and laugh as the children fought for it. I had seen jolly ranchers passed out at velocity via a slingshot. Leaving welts for just a small lump of sugar. On the other side, it was not uncommon for the children to be hit and sent sprawling, while the adults stole what was clearly meant for children.

All of that aside, we occasionally were able to accomplish some good. We gave out boxes of school supplies and helped build infrastructure buildings like wells or irrigation systems. We also worked in concert with other humanitarian agencies in the area. The predominant one being the U.N.

A mission gone south had soured the locals on us for a time. As a result, the U.N. decided it would be safer to forgo the usual complement of soldiers to act as security. Instead, opting on their better image and own poorly trained security force.

It took thirteen minutes for them to be hit. Three suicide bombers. Men dressed in blue burqas pretending to be women. The security responsible for letting them through didn't live long enough to regret it as moments after the initial explosion, a vehicle borne IED had them paying the ultimate price for their laxity.

We arrived on the scene in minutes, but the damage was already done. I had arrived to what I personally can only describe as a hellscape. The acrid smell of explosives combined with the smell of burning flesh. A haze still lingered in the air as if even the sky itself was trying to cover up this sin.

This brings us to the thing I didn't tell you. The vitally important piece of information to really drive home the barbarity of it all. What the aid was. Gardez, in conjunction with the U.N. was opening an elementary school that little girls would be able to attend. They were passing out the books and papers that would be needed for class as well as food and clothing to those who needed it.

Children's bodies were strewn about like ragdolls at daycare after a particularly long day of play. The worst part was, they weren't all dead. Their cries and moans permeated the air. The unmistakable sound of human agony transcends language. Seemingly each sense bringing some fresh hell to bear.

I write this knowing I won't be able to sleep tonight. Just the thought is enough to drive me back to a bottle. It is important that their stories are told though. So, like my chosen profession, I too must soldier on.

Triage stations were set. The medics saved who they could and made comfortable those they could not (I have an intense mix of admiration and hate for those with the ability to black tag a child. Essentially, they had to say that this child is functionally dead, and we need to spend our time with people we could still save.) We pushed out and secured the area. Pieces of the bombers were found. The explosion caused by a bomb vest does peculiar things to a human body. The hands and feet are detached at the joints. The skin from the head detaches almost intact. While I couldn't say for certain this holds true for every case. It held true for the ones I saw. We took the time to fingerprint the bodies. Evidence was gathered. This eventually leads us to the bomb maker, but not that day. I vomited several times, but each time returned to mission. I owed it to the girls.

We took two U.N. people back with us for safety. One, a dark-haired female who didn't say much, just stared blankly at the wall on the inside of my truck. The other a fat gentleman who would not stop talking to me in French. I don't know what he said as I do not know any French. The only reason I stressed that he was fat, is because he had two flak jackets tied together to try and cover his massive girth. Funny what the mind remembers. I didn't know this man, but I knew he had just been through a tragedy. He had witnessed something that shook him to his very core. I also knew that I hated him. *How can you let this happen? Didn't you know that the enemy is out there? Why didn't you let us do our job? We could have protected you, we could have protected those girls. You fat fuck. This is your fault.* I handed him a bag of M&Ms I had been saving. With equal parts compassion and disgust I watched him eat the bag. This at least shut him up for a while. I was happy to see him go.

On the way out, we found one last piece of evidence. The face of one of the bombers. Our driver swore he didn't mean to run it over. I didn't believe him. Pieces were stuck in the tire when we got back. We donned gloves and cleaned it the best we could. Throwing whatever we could into a fire. A silent prayer was sent with the smoke, I hope his soul was burning too. Bastard.

To this day, I have a hard time around full body burkas. I also cannot abide the taste of plain M&Ms. A scar left not on my body, but on my soul.

Point

What is the point, reader? Why are we reliving this? Why? Why…

Afterword

My name is Richard Dawson. I served with then Spc. LeClaire during his Afghanistan deployment. Rodney James LeClaire was found dead by his wife on the morning of May 31, 2020. It would have been his 33rd birthday. He is survived by his wife of eleven years and his ten-year-old son. The cause of death; self-inflicted gunshot, apparent suicide. This manuscript was found among his effects. It was his wife's wish that I distribute this among the other veterans.

While I do not have his gift for words, it is my hope that maybe you can gain some understanding. Veteran suicide is a constant and continued threat. At this point, I have lost more friends to suicide, than to enemy combatants.

LeClaire was always quick with the laugh and ready to help a friend in need. He would mock you for being poor, while feeding you from his own plate. He is missed. Rest easy, dear friend. May you find peace in death that eluded you in life.

If you or someone you know is suffering from PTSD please be aware of the resources that exist around you. Veterans suffering mental health emergencies can always go to the veteran crisis line. www.veteranscrisisline.com or 1-800-273-8255- press one.

Others can seek out the national suicide hotline at 1-800-273-8255.

SHAMELESS PLEA FROM AUTHOR

Hey if you enjoyed the book, or even if you didn't, please take a few minutes to leave me a review on Amazon. A lot of people only buy based off of the reviews.

If you want to contact me you can do so at anthony_lecours@protonmail.com. I can fix any mistakes that might have slipped through the cracks. Otherwise, I'd be happy to answer any questions, or just be there if you need to vent.

Finally, you can also check out my Facebook page if you search for AJ Lecours. It is here where I will hopefully post up my follow up novel. PTSME Too.

Finally, (for real this time) thank you. I am probably never going to be able to be a full time novelist, but it means a lot for you to invite me into your home, and let me tell you my story.

Made in United States
Cleveland, OH
16 February 2025

14419096R00135